TREGARN AUTUMN

TREGARN AUTUMN

Dee Wyatt

Chivers Press • **Thorndike Press**
Bath, England **Waterville, Maine USA**

This Large Print edition is published by Chivers Press, England, and by Thorndike Press, USA.

Published in 2002 in the U.K. by arrangement with Robert Hale.

Published in 2002 in the U.S. by arrangement with Robert Hale Limited.

U.K. Hardcover ISBN 0–7540–4928–0 (Chivers Large Print)
U.S. Softcover   ISBN 0–7862–4255–8 (Nightingale Series Edition)

The text of this Large Print edition is unabridged.
Other aspects of the book may vary from the original edition.

Set in 16 pt. New Times Roman.

Printed in Great Britain on acid-free paper.

British Library Cataloguing in Publication Data available

Library of Congress Cataloging-in-Publication Data

Wyatt, Dee
　　　Tregarn autumn / Dee Wyatt.
　　　　　p.　　cm.
　　　ISBN 0–7862–4255–8 (lg. print : sc : alk. paper)
　　　1. Administration of estates—Fiction. 2. Divorced women—
Fiction. 3. Large type books. I. Title.
PR6073.Y32 T74 2002
823'.914—dc21　　　　　　　　　　　　　　　　2002024173

CHAPTER ONE

Hannah Jones's blue eyes were thoughtful as she turned the car into the quiet road that would take her home to Tregarn. The daylight had faded now and the blossoming trees along the sides of the road were becoming an indistinct blur in the evening's soft shadows. Through the Volvo's half-open window, the light, sweet-scented breeze ruffled her dark hair, but Hannah didn't even notice. The beauty of Tregarn meant nothing to her tonight. For two pins she would sell up and be done with it—the temptation was very strong. It didn't seem fair that she should be saddled with such a responsibility as this.

Hannah sighed. She knew that, even if she did go away, it wouldn't do any good. Besides, where could she go? She had already sold anything that was of any value—everything, that is, except the house. And the house was her only refuge now.

Hannah smiled ruefully to herself. Somehow she had to get things into perspective again. She was facing an uphill task and acting like this—feeling sorry for herself—wasn't doing any good at all. There must be *something* she could salvage from the financial disaster she found herself in.

She glanced across the hazy fields. She

preferred this route. Since the advent of the motorway most people avoided the narrow, twisting B-road, opting for the efficiency of speed to the breathtaking scenery that lay on both sides of her now.

There was never any traffic along here and she rarely had need of her rear-view mirror, so it was with a small jerk of surprise that she noticed the car behind her. Even then, she hardly gave it a glance as it manoeuvred to pass her on the bend, cutting so close that she had to swerve to give it more room. She was even more surprised when the car didn't overtake and moved into the side of the road with her.

She threw a hurried cursory look as it braked then backed up ready to swing into her again.

'Look out!' she yelled angrily, yanking the steering wheel further to her left.

She was too late! There was no escaping the grinding sound of metal as the car hit her!

Hannah slammed on the brakes as she felt the nearside wheels sink into the soft, muddy ditch, the other car still ramming against her. She pulled viciously on the wheel, wrestling hard, too angry and too scared now to even scream at the other driver. Then suddenly, the other car pulled away, shooting off down the road and out of sight, leaving Hannah shaking like a leaf and braking hard on the Volvo.

She leaned her head against the wheel.

What kind of idiot was that? Was it some demented joyrider out for kicks? Damn! She hadn't even thought to take his number.

She jerked her head up quickly as the screech of tyres came again. The lunatic must have made a U-turn further on because there was no doubt in Hannah's mind that he was coming back.

The Granada was making straight for her. Metallic silver, and a man at the wheel. She couldn't see his face, there was something covering it—a knitted hood or a ski mask— and, suddenly, the coldness of fear was back.

Hannah acted instinctively, as though her life depended on it. The Granada swerved towards her again and she swung wildly, this time to her right, as the other car hit her rear wing. The contact sent the Volvo spinning into a terrifying half circle before sliding off the road again and into the verge, scraping against one of the tall poplar trees.

Her car bogged down into the oozy mud and Hannah could hear herself yelling incoherently at the other car. Dazed, her head lolled back against her seat, faintness threatening to overwhelm her as she forced herself to think. Her brain felt numb, stunned and foggy, but she knew she must not lose control and, after a moment, instinct took over. She released the safety belt, groping, trying to open the door but finding it jammed against the tree.

3

Looking round wildly for signs of the Granada, she threw herself across the seat to open the other door, pushing against it and tumbling out in the same motion. Numbly, Hannah dragged herself out, crouching by the rear bumper and trying to listen for sounds of the other car above her tortuous breathing.

She couldn't hear a thing. Please, dear Lord, had the madman gone? Cautiously, she peered along the road, thankful to find that it was deserted now and, still trembling from shock, Hannah straightened up. She steadied herself, taking a few deep breaths and trying to calm down as she leaned against the battered side of the Volvo.

Who on earth would try to run her off the road like that? Who was the maniac who could so easily have killed her? Pity the light had been too faint to take his number, but, number or not, the first thing she would do when she got home would be to ring the police. A madman like that needed putting away!

*　　　*　　　*

Hannah Jones drained the last of her coffee and glanced at her watch. She was feeling a little better. She had telephoned the police station and the sergeant had been most sympathetic. Had she been hurt? Had she taken the Granada's number? Just where had the accident taken place? Hannah had

4

answered as best she could and was told not to worry. They would send someone over for more details. They would find the Granada.

Hannah sighed. Her car was a wreck. The collision with the Granada had been the last thing she needed right now. Life had been far from easy this last year and her nerves were already at snapping point. It was hardly surprising. Everything had gone wrong! Paul's irrational, unfounded jealousy and his extravagant life-style had almost destroyed her. Now, she was free! But, free or not, she had enough to worry about keeping Tregarn's head above water without brooding about some crazy drunk who treated the road like a fairground.

'Better pull yourself together, Hannah girl,' she muttered to herself. 'Putting up with a nutcase is nothing compared to what you have to face next.'

Hannah chewed on her bottom lip and glanced again at her watch. It told her it was a little after half past nine—still early. Chris Talbot would still be up. Hannah sat silently thoughtful for a few moments, then taking a deep, bracing breath, she got up and leafed through the directory for his number. But even as she depressed the pushbuttons the inevitable reaction set in.

A woman's voice answered after a couple of rings.

'Seven-nine-six, Talbot Twr Gwyn . . .

5

Megan Davies speaking . . .'

Hannah's voice was amazingly cool. 'I'd like to speak to Chris, Megan, is he around?'

'I'm sorry, I'm afraid not,' the woman came back. 'He's asked not to be disturbed. May I take a message?'

'Megan, it's me, Hannah Jones, and it's very important that I speak to him. Would you make an exception just this once and ask him to come to the phone?'

There was the slightest hesitation before the woman's voice came back again. 'Oh, hello Hannah. I'd heard you were back at Tregarn. But I'm not sure that Chris'll take very kindly to being disturbed tonight, it would be better to ring him in the morning.'

Hannah wasn't at all that surprised to hear he was too busy to be disturbed. It had to be some woman he was entertaining. His reputation was notorious in the small town of Tregarn and Chris Talbot's close encounters of the female kind well acknowledged.

'No, Megan, it really *is* vital that I speak to him . . . please . . . see what you can do.'

'Well, . . all right, I'll try, but don't blame me if he bites your head off.'

Hearing the clicking sound as the woman transferred her call sent Hannah's pulse racing even more than it already was and, as she heard the sound of the receiver being picked up at the other end, her throat seemed to close up stifling her breathing.

6

'Talbot.' His deep, slightly impatient voice came down the line, making her hand tighten even more around the receiver.

Here we go, she thought, breathing deeply. 'Hello! Hannah Jones here.' She prayed her voice sounded cool as she went on. 'There's something I need to discuss with you.'

'You've caught me at a bad time, I haven't time for anything right now. We have a mare in foal and I'm waiting to hear from the vet. What is it you want?'

Hannah bristled. So she was wrong! It wasn't a woman after all. Nevertheless, his manner was far from agreeable and she continued equally curtly, 'What I have to say will take more than a minute. Perhaps it would be better if I made an appointment to see you when—when you're not so tied up. Perhaps I could come over to Twr Gwyn tomorrow?'

She heard his short, humourless laugh. 'Tomorrow's just as bad. I run a stable of thoroughbreds and they need constant attention, I haven't time for socializing.'

'Then when?'

She heard him mutter an impatient curse. 'I can't say—'

'It's very important.'

He gave an audible sigh. 'How important?'

'I need to talk to you about the land my father sold to you.'

There was a moment's hesitation before he came back sourly, 'What about it?'

7

'I want to buy it back.'

'Forget it! Besides, from what I hear, you haven't got the wherewithal to buy it back anyway, and I'm not in the charity business.'

Anger leaped inside her, swift and hot. She wanted to tell him to go to blazes but she knew she was in no position to do that now, so instead of lashing him with her tongue as she usually did, she said contritely, 'May we discuss it when you're not too busy? It's important to both of us and it needs talking about face to face.'

Again a small pause before he came back, 'Well, it may be of importance to you, but it certainly isn't to me. I can't think of a thing we have to talk about.' There was another short pause before he added in a bored, long-suffering tone, 'But never let it be said that I'm not a good neighbour; I suppose I could spare a few minutes tomorrow evening—I have an appointment in Tregarn town in the afternoon so it's not out of my way. Will that do? Say about seven?'

'Fine . . .' Hannah expelled a breath she hadn't known she was holding. 'Seven o'clock will be fine.'

He hung up immediately and Hannah replaced the receiver with an impatient jerk. At least she'd broken the ice, but their brief discussion only confirmed her belief that his manners hadn't improved much since they'd last met.

She flopped back in her chair and unfolded the rather crumpled slip of paper in her hand, her blue eyes drifting once more to the single paragraph at the bottom of the page.

Her best land! Twenty-four of the most arable acres on Tregarn had been handed over just like that! Hannah mentally clicked her fingers. And for what? Why had her father done it? And without a word to her! Christian Langley Talbot had bought the prettiest part of the whole estate and she hadn't been told a thing about it!

She couldn't bring herself to read any more. Instead she thrust the paper back into the drawer of the desk and closed her eyes against the wave of angry frustration. Why did it have to be him? Chris Talbot of all people? Why not one of their other neighbours? It wouldn't have made any difference of course, the end result would be the same. She would still be without the land she needed so desperately if she was to turn Tregarn into the successful hotel she wanted it to be. But at least she would have been spared the humiliation of asking him such a favour. The thought of that made her insides shrink. She shrugged inwardly. Well at least he was willing to see her, and there was nothing more she could do tonight.

Hannah went upstairs and took a quick shower. Tired as she was, when she got into bed she couldn't sleep. The accident earlier had upset her more than she realized and that—along with the prospect of talking to Chris Talbot tomorrow—filled her mind, sending any thoughts of sleep a long way away.

Christian Langley Talbot. He floated into her mind's eye. If only he wasn't so tall, or so damned attractive! If only he wasn't so blond-haired . . . or brown-eyed . . . or broad-shouldered! She had always felt threatened by him! She had never felt like that with Paul—or any other man if it came to that—and it angered her.

Chris Talbot had no right to excite her in this strange, primitive way. The two families—the Joneses and the Talbots—had known each other all their lives—they were neighbours and their parents had been friends. But, lying there against the pillows, her mind drifted to when she'd been sixteen and they'd had their first real clash of wills; to the time of her first really important social event—the annual Christmas dance at the village hall. And although she hadn't realized it then, it had been the first time she had seen Chris Talbot through a woman's eyes; seen him no longer as the boy next door but as the man he'd become.

Hannah's cheeks grew hot as she remembered her barefaced insolence. He had walked through the door, looking first to his left and then to his right, at last turning her way. And when Hannah saw his face on that evening, she had instantly fallen in love.

That had been her first mistake. And her second one had been to imagine that Christian Langley Talbot would ever return her love.

Charlie Jones's spoiled, pampered only child had been brought up to believe that the world lay at her feet, and she only had to crook her finger to make everything fall into her lap. Hannah's callow heart had reasoned that if she had fallen in love with Chris at first sight, then surely he must fall in love with her too, even though he had eyes only for the girl in the blue dress standing a few yards away, a girl Hannah had never seen before.

With an almost pathetic eagerness she'd edged nearer to him, trying to catch his eye until, standing close enough to touch him, she had stared fixedly at his profile, willing him to turn and look at her.

At last, his eyes briefly flickering, he had returned her gaze, saying quietly, 'If you spend the entire evening staring at me like that you'll end up with a crick in your neck.'

Hannah winced, startled by his mockery. He wasn't supposed to react like this. He should have been swept off his feet the moment his eyes met hers and this snub was the first really painful experience of her young life, and it hurt so much she wanted to hurt back.

'Don't flatter yourself,' she retorted hotly to cover her embarrassment. 'I wasn't staring at you, I was—I was looking at that picture on the wall.'

'Really?' he murmured, his eyes drifting to the dusty, faded portrait of some long-gone village stalwart, 'I hadn't realized old man Reece was so interesting.' The line of his mouth curved upwards in amused condescension as he turned back again, eyeing her up and down. 'My, my, how you've grown up. It must be two years since I last saw you. You *are* Charlie Jones's girl, aren't you?'

'Yes, I'm Hannah.'

'I thought you were still at school.'

'I am.'

'Are you home for good now?'

'Of course not!' Hannah had answered airily. 'I'll never come home for good again—it's too boring here!'

'I see . . . and would it be too *boring* to ask you to dance?'

He had turned to look at her full on then and Hannah had felt her mouth go dry as the dark eyes seemed to examine every inch of her. She had shrugged haughtily. 'No, I don't care to, thank you.' No one had ever made her feel so clumsy and gauche before and she wanted to add petulantly, 'And I wouldn't dance with you now if you were the last man on earth!' She didn't, but from now on she would dance with every man in the room! That is everyone but *him*!

'Suit yourself,' he had commented drily, his gaze still moving over her. 'You're not a bad-looking kid; it's a pity you spoil your face by pouting so much.'

There was something about him that was bringing out the worst in her and her peevishness spilled out uncontrollably. 'I don't need your opinion, thank you! You're just like all the rest of the boys around here . . . unsophisticated!'

Chris Talbot's expression had hardened just a fraction. 'Your expensive school clearly hasn't taught you good manners,' he remarked after a brief pause, adding softly, 'You must be the rudest girl I've ever met, and it'll give me great pleasure to take you down a peg or two one of these days . . .'

'I don't need anyone to take me down, especially someone like you—I like it up here!'

'If you'll excuse me.' His glance flickered back to the girl in the blue dress, throwing Hannah one last vague look that confirmed his distaste of her. 'I have more interesting things to do. See you around some time—my regards to your father.'

Hannah had flounced away. She knew she had acted in a childishly rude and offensive way, and yet she was also aware, even then, of the sensuality of Chris Talbot. Somehow, his tall, proud, masculinity reminded Hannah of the power of her favourite horse.

Young as she was, she recognized his aura of authority. There wasn't a more handsome man in the place and, as he'd murmured something to the girl in blue, her heart seemed

13

to stop beating for a moment. She'd been only sixteen and he was already twenty-one. She had been too young and too naive to understand her reactions and it had frightened her.

Somehow, knowing he disliked her so much made her feel better, and that was how she'd wanted it ever since. He'd turned from Hannah to the more agreeable attentions of the girl in blue, dismissing her as the indulged, rude little minx she was, and from that evening they'd got off on the wrong foot and Hannah had never tried to change the situation between them.

She *never* wanted that formidable sensuality of his turned on her.

Yet it was inevitable in a place as small as Tregarn town that their paths would cross again, and whenever they did she'd been as toffee-nosed as she possibly could. Over the next two or three years, whenever she'd been home and he'd called at Tregarn to see her father about something or other, she treated him so much like dirt that even her mother rebuked her for it. But Hannah didn't care. A hostile distance was safer where Christian Langley Talbot was concerned.

After her mother died and her father had seemed to lose interest in anything except Tregarn, Hannah had decided on a life of her own. She had left her home for the glitter of the city and the glamour of opening her own antiques shop. But that had been when she'd made her third mistake! The worst disaster of her life! Within a year she had met and married Paul Denton!

*   *   *

At last Hannah fell into a restless sleep and when morning came she loitered over breakfast. She looked out of the kitchen window at the hazy blur of the rhododendron bushes flowering along the drive, bright in the morning's light and drawing her heart from its shadows.

'Oh Dad . . . Dad . . . why did you have to leave me, too?'

She loved her home. She hadn't realised just how much until she'd come back here with Paul after her father died. Now Tregarn was all she had left. It was her soul and she always felt safe here. Tregarn House had represented everything her father ever dreamed of. It wasn't particularly an architectural gem. It belonged to no particular period. In fact, to some it looked like an over-iced cake and seemed ugly with its extravagant embellishment. But there was also something incredibly soothing about it and, without those twenty-four acres, it seemed amputated. She knew she would find some way to get those acres back—to make it whole again.

Eventually, she wandered out into the

grounds. The day was already too hot and humid, heavy with the promise of a storm. Hannah shaded her eyes with her hand, looking across the sweep of the lawn at the new hothouse. It gleamed majestically in the too-bright morning sun as it waited patiently for its display of exotic flora. Further on, beyond the row of poplars, two workmen were already at their task of laying the new tennis courts.

Hannah leaned her arms against the balustrade, concentrating her thoughts on what to do. How on earth would she raise more money to pay for all this? And how should she approach Chris Talbot? It would all depend on the talk she was to have with him—and the bank!

Her promise to her father, that she would complete his dream of turning Tregarn into a holiday centre, was becoming more and more difficult to keep. It had grown out of all proportion. At first it had started as a country hotel, ideal for climbers situated as it was in the foothills of the Black Mountains, and perfect for families in its idyllic setting by Rhysnant Lake and Celli Forest.

But, since Paul's grandiose ideas of including a conference centre as well—and all the new building that that project had involved, the money had slipped through his fingers like grains of sand. She had been a fool to leave it to him! Her father had warned her of his erratic ways with money—and women! She should have known that when the money ran out her husband would leave her for more glamorous, richer pickings. To survive, Hannah had sold every asset she owned—her jewellery—her antiques. Everything. Even her car had had to go—sensibly swopping the expensive Porsche for the battered, twelve-year-old Volvo. Now that had gone too! Her family. Her security. Her marriage. Everything!

Hannah sighed wearily. She was determined to make it succeed. Those twenty-four acres were vital. With three-quarters of the project already completed, the land was needed for guest bungalows if Tregarn was to open to the public by next summer. And, if she was to survive, next summer's opening was the crucial deadline.

CHAPTER TWO

A little before seven o'clock the threatened storm broke out. Sitting in the study going over her estimate papers for the hundredth time Hannah glanced out of the window. Hearing the low rumble of thunder, she got up to draw the curtains and, as her hand touched on the faded brown velvet, the lights of Chris Talbot's Colt Shogun turned into the drive.

Sheets of rain were already sluicing down the windshield and, in dim light of the courtyard, there was no mistaking the dark ill-humour of his countenance. Even through the rain she saw that he glanced around him, taking in the new mish-mash of buildings around the courtyard, and she was aware of his disdain as he drew nearer the house. His expression said it all. The Queen Bee was indulging in another one of her ridiculous, costly whims!

He was drenched by the time he ran up the narrow flight of steps and Hannah opened the door to him just as he lifted his hand to ring the bell. Rivulets of rain ran off his black leather jacket, making small pools around his feet and, as Hannah's blue eyes met his, she recognized the old familiar look of repressed dislike.

She hesitated for just a moment, almost reluctant to let him in, and then she pushed the door open wider. 'Come in.'

'Thanks.'

There was no smile of welcome on her face and, unless he was as deaf as a post, he couldn't fail to hear the ice in her voice as she stepped back to close the door after him.

He took off his dripping tweed cap. She'd forgotten how tall he was. And everything about him suggested money. Even in the black leather jacket he looked as though he belonged in a corporate boardroom rather than in the countryside. He looked like a man who made multi-million-pound deals for some merchant bank instead of breeding race horses for a living, and all the physical work it entailed.

Hannah's face was set. It was going to choke her to be nice to him, but she tried not to let her thoughts show on her face as he stepped past her. 'Let's go into Dad's study, it's warmer in there.'

Chris followed her down the hall. As she led him through she tried to collect her thoughts. She was far too aware of him as he walked beside her along the corridor; aware of a physical closeness that made her keep her chin high and her voice firm. She wasn't going to let him see how much he affected her. She was a mature businesswoman, involved in the task of converting the old farm of Tregarn into an up-market, paying concern. Yet, with true feminine illogicality, she was glad she'd spent more time than usual over her dress. At least she didn't *look* like Little Orphan Annie, even though she felt like her!

Hannah moved on silently, leading him along the passage and feeling confident in the floating, wide-legged black trousers and white silk shirt. Her black hair was pulled back and fastened with a gold clip at the nape of her neck.

'Please . . .' She opened the study door, indicating with a sweep of her hand a chair by

19

the desk. 'I know you're a busy man so let's not waste any time. I suppose you know why I want to see you.'

His expression hardened. 'I have a pretty good idea.'

She moved behind the desk, sitting down in her father's chair. 'I found the paper my Dad signed selling you the twenty-four acres by Rhysnant Lake . . .' She glanced up, pausing for a moment in case he wanted to say something. There was no emotion in her voice as she studied his face and no one looking at her could guess how much she was hating this. He merely shrugged so she went on, 'I need those acres back.'

'No way.'

Hannah gritted her teeth. 'I fully intend to pay you back, plus a reasonable profit of course. It's just—' She cleared her throat. 'It's just that right now I haven't quite the amount to do so.'

'I've told you I don't want to sell.' His voice was deceptively casual.

'But you have lots of land, surely you managed without my twenty-four acres before.'

'I'm not selling. And I don't see the point of this discussion, especially when you've no means to pay me anyway.'

Hannah stared across at him. Even over the short distance he was too close and the look in his eyes made her shiver. 'I was hoping we could come to some agreement.'

Strangely, her words seemed to amuse him. Chris Talbot threw back his blond head and laughed, chuckling for several moments before he finally subsided, his dark eyes throwing her an oddly challenging look. 'Now I'm interested. What kind of agreement did you have in mind?'

Hannah gave a small shrug. 'I'm sure there must be something I could do for you.'

He laughed even more. 'Oh, yes . . . you're damn right there is. There's always been something you could do for me.'

Hannah's blue eyes widened. She hadn't expected such a rapid and promising response and his words had stopped her in her tracks.

She shot him another look, heart beating, mind racing. 'Then name it.' Laughing a little nervously she added, 'I must say that comes as a relief.'

'I think we're talking about two different things.' Suddenly the laughter was gone, he was at once serious and businesslike. 'But to get back to basics, that land is mine now, I bought it fairly and squarely from your father and I'm not selling it back just like that.' He waved a dismissive hand in the air. 'And certainly not for some hare-brained scheme like your hotel and conference centre.'

Hannah sucked in her breath. He was delighting in his advantage of power over her, making her pay for all the nasty little digs

21

she'd laid into him over the years, and for all the other things he disliked about her. 'You might at least consider it,' she said calmly. 'After all, the hotel was my father's idea too; he must have told you about it.'

He sat back, spreading his long legs out before him and eyeing her quizzically. 'Yes, he told me, but your father didn't intend turning the whole valley into a visitor centre the way you are. And I have the feeling you're getting out of your depth.'

She held his gaze squarely, admitting with painful honesty, 'At the moment, yes, perhaps it does seem a little—'she coughed delicately—'a little ambitious. But Paul—' She stopped herself, clearing her throat. 'I know exactly what I'm doing and those Rhysnant acres are extremely necessary to me if I'm to open next summer.'

'Paul? Your husband?'

'My ex-husband—we're divorced.'

'Ah, yes . . . I remember. And what's happened to him, Mrs Denton?'

'Ms Jones. I've reverted back to Jones.'

'Ah, yes,' he repeated. 'Someone mentioned that to me, too.'

Hannah cleared her throat again. 'Paul drew up many plans for this place—raised investment—so you see, it wasn't only my hare-brained scheme. My ex-husband was—is—an architect and knows a good deal when he sees one.'

Hannah regarded him stonily, ignoring the amused, quirked eyebrow and waited. She regarded the handsome face and the expression that was both cool and polite, and did not know why she should be feeling such a sense of unease.

'And how much experience has your architect ex-husband had on this kind of project?'

Hannah lifted her chin. 'He's had a great deal to do with conversions—Cardiff Docklands, for instance.'

There was a touch of mockery in his tone. 'Then where is he now? Doesn't he intend to see his project through?'

'No. He's—busy with other things now.'

'I see.' Chris Talbot's eyes were like dark hollows. 'And he's dropped everything in your lap?'

Hannah looked away briefly, avoiding his gaze and hoping she appeared to be unconcerned. 'It was a mutual arrangement.'

Talbot eyed her thoughtfully. 'Who else has money tied up in Tregarn?'

'The bank, of course.' Her answer came a little unsteadily. Hannah stared at him across the desk. He was enjoying this. He was deliberately making her squirm. But common sense also prevailed and she knew that no matter what, until she got back her land, she had to keep on the right side of this man.

He stared at her for a long time, then he

said quietly and unexpectedly, 'Suppose I came in on the deal . . .'

Hannah's blue eyes widened and her mouth dropped open in astonishment. 'You? In what way?'

'Suppose I put some money into it,' he went on, his dark eyes full of gravity now.

'But—'

'What's the matter? Why are you so surprised? Does that idea repel you so much? He laughed softly. 'But, of course, I'd forgotten, you can't stand people like me to crawl from under stones!'

Hannah fought back her reflexes. What was he suggesting? What was he up to? 'Why—why would you want to do that? Why can't you just sell me back my land and have done with it?'

'Because I have a better idea.'

After a moment's thought, she retorted stiffly, 'And that is?'

Chris Talbot laughed, eyeing her closely. 'Let's face it, you haven't a great deal of choice, have you? As I see it, there isn't a thing you can deny me and, heaven knows, I've waited long enough!' He shot a disparaging look at the expression on her face, adding quietly, 'But, if my coming into it is too repugnant to contemplate, then don't worry, I wouldn't dream of forcing you.' He regarded her again and she saw her worst fears were verified when he spoke again and she saw the finite edge of anger glittering in his eyes. 'But I promise you this, my coming into the project will be the only way you'll get those bungalows built. Take it or leave it.' He stood up, picking up his leather jacket from where he'd thrown it across a chair. 'Anyway, it's late and I still have a lot to do at home. We'll talk about it tomorrow.' He laughed again. 'When you've had time to chew it over.'

Hannah made a small impatient movement with her right hand, stalling for time, her fingers twitching nervously around the dial of her watch. 'But why should you invest in Tregarn?' The idea was so ridiculous that she almost laughed in his face as she waited for him to go on.

'It's just an idea,' he went on quietly, his eyes narrowed into slits. He shifted in the chair, crossing his long legs. 'But it might work, in spite of knowing the kind of person you are.'

Hannah stared at him, bewilderment and frustration crossing her face. 'If that's your only solution to my request,' she snapped, 'then you can forget it!' How she was hating the unpalatable truth of her situation. 'I was hoping for a more serious discussion with you.'

There was a pause and he leaned across the space between them, reaching his hand to her face and stroking her cheek with his index finger. Hannah jerked her head away, feeling her throat contract as she responded to his touch in spite of everything. And angry with herself at her response; for knowing him as the womanizer he was.

'I am serious, Hannah Jones,' he said quietly. 'Very serious.'

'You—you can't be! Why on earth would you be interested in coming into something you so obviously despise? It's—it's not like you . . . it's not—not businesslike!' She made the point far more calmly than she felt.

He stood up, moving towards the door, turning as he opened it. 'Oh, I'm interested, and even though I despise the idea as you so readily point out, it will certainly be businesslike, have no fear about that. You and I can't be anything other than businesslike, can we?'

She had moved to stand beside him. As she looked up, his face was so close to hers that she could see in his eyes the gold flecks around each iris. But there was also a biting sarcasm in his question and it caught her off guard.

She shook her head brusquely, trying desperately to keep her mind off the broadness of his shoulders and on to the main purpose of their meeting. 'No, we can't. And of course, I'm willing to hear more of your idea—'

'Do you have a choice?' He gave her a disarming smile, unperturbed by her angry face and which only served to antagonize her more. Then Chris Talbot laughed and opened the door, and before she could question him further he was already making his way down the hall and towards the door.

CHAPTER THREE

Hannah made no move. His words refused to make sense and she tried to convince herself she'd heard him wrongly. When he reached the door he turned, regarding her with that odd expression on his face, threatening, making her feel second-rate as he always did.

Then his words realigned themselves in her head and panic took over. She ran forward quickly, saying as she reached him, 'You're joking, of course!' But as soon as she'd said it she knew it was no joke. Her stomach tightened and she lifted her head in a haughty stare. 'You can't possibly be serious!'

His face was hard and still, his eyes narrowed as he watched her. His voice came down to her, his tone too soft . . . dangerous . . . 'I assure you, I mean every word I say. No partnership—no bungalows.'

The implication of his words took her breath away. She had fought him all these years and she wasn't about to weaken now; wasn't about to crumple to his demand for the sake of a few bungalows. There *must* be another way.

Hannah responded quickly, her face burning with fury and her voice scathing. 'That's blackmail!'

'Take it or leave it.'

'I'll—I'll—There are other things to consider!' She moved to pass him to open the door but he was too quick for her. He jerked towards her, gripping her upper arm with his lean, sinewy hand. She saw only too clearly the rage that was spurring him now. Perhaps it was the way she was looking at him—as though he was nothing more than an insect to be despised—and she didn't even try to disguise the contempt in her face. It was her way of showing Christian Talbot that even the mere thought of having him as a partner in Tregarn was too unbearable to even contemplate.

'Don't turn your nose up at me, Miss High-and-Mighty! You need me in case you haven't noticed.' He gave a grim laugh. 'But by all means, talk it over with your ex-husband and partner if he's still involved. Just tell him what I've told you, no deal—no bungalows.'

Hannah realized she was shaking. His touch was sending shock waves through her system. 'What possible interest could you have in Tregarn? she asked scathingly. 'Haven't you enough to do at Twr Gwyn without complicating my life more than it is already?'

He watched her closely, as though he was trying to see what lay in her thoughts. 'Your complicated life is your problem, not mine. And talking of complications, what went wrong with your marriage? Couldn't he stand the pace?'

'None of that's anything to do with you.'

'On the contrary,' he said quietly, 'it's everything to do with me now that you need my help.'

Hannah was goaded, her voice snapping, 'You're impossible! I should have known better than to ask for your help. I should have known I'd get no consideration from *you*!'

'Why not from me?' he asked, his brown eyes narrowed and angry. 'If my memory serves me right, I'm the only one who really knows what goes on inside that lovely head of yours. Besides, I'm probably the only one who can afford you.'

'I'm not for sale!'

'It's perhaps as well because I'm not buying,' he murmured sarcastically, gripping her arm and his face so close to hers his breath fanned against her forehead. 'I'm only renting a little time with you.' He gave a low, ironic laugh but she could hear no humour in it. 'Let's just say I'm intrigued with whatever it is you're cooking up for Tregarn and, in my warped way, I'd like to be part of it.'

Hannah made a small inarticulate gasp of protest and wrenched her arm away. This was the first time they had ever really touched each other and the feeling he was starting inside her was more than fear. It was something far deeper than that, and it frightened her even more. She'd always felt instinctively that she wouldn't be able to handle him.

He gripped her chin between his thumb and

forefinger, his eyes staring down into her own. His expression shook her. Hannah was used to men looking at her, but no man had ever looked at her the way Chris Talbot was looking at her now. There was the light of pure sexual speculation in his eyes and it was even more frightening because of her own insidious reaction.

Until her father died, she had never been alone—not *really* alone! Hannah had never been responsible for her own destiny. Now this man was enticing her. Somehow, she had to conquer this bewitchment. Whatever the outcome she had to fight Chris Talbot this time on her own. She had to prove to herself that he meant nothing to her! That she was no Trilby to his, oh-so-seductive, Svengali.

Slowly, as if his muscles ached, he let his hand loosen and she eased away from him to lean against the wall. Hannah averted her eyes, not wanting him to see the expression on her face, not wanting to betray by even a flicker that she'd liked the way his touch had awakened this demon deep down inside her.

Pride became her ally as she said softly, 'As I've already told you, I—we—haven't the money to buy back the land right now but I'll find it from somewhere. There's no need for you to involve yourself personally in Tregarn. All I'm asking is that you'll think about selling back those twenty-four acres. I'm asking for your co-operation and—'

'I've already told you my terms,' he interrupted, his eyes narrowing at her coolness.

She continued doggedly, 'I need that land for the bungalows. I must have the accommodation one hundred percent ready by next summer, otherwise, I lose everything. If you insist on holding on to it then I'll have to look for an alternative and time's running out. Please—please be reasonable and say that you'll think about it.'

Slowly he straightened up, his brows drawing together as he looked down at her. 'What alternative?'

She shrugged. 'I—I would have to look for some other piece of land.'

'And where would you find it?' The exasperation in his tone was evident. 'Tregarn and Twr Gwyn are the only estates for miles with that amount of acreage. Would you expect your tourists to take the train into Cardiff or Swansea and spend the night there?'

Hannah persisted. 'I'd find something. I have to if I'm going to break even.'

Chris Talbot broke in impatiently, 'Hold on a minute! You're living in cloud-cuckoo land. Are you trying to tell me that you really believe that by building those bungalows by next summer you can attract enough tourists to break even? That you can really turn this place into a going concern—a tourist attraction—in so short a time?'

31

'Yes, I am,' she countered, stubbornness creeping into her tone.

'Then you're a bigger fool than I took you for.' His disbelief was evident.

'I'm not interested in your personal opinion of me.'

'To run Tregarn in the way you're talking about needs a professional and you can't even run a second hand shop.'

'Yes I can! And it was an *antiques* business!' Her eyes held his now, angry and proud. 'And I can be as professional as anyone! I'm determined to see this project through!'

Chris looked her up and down, his brows lifting as he surveyed her. There was even a hint of amusement playing round his mouth. 'All by yourself?'

'Yes.' Hannah stood with her lips pressed together in a grim line. There was even a touch of grudging admiration in his manner towards her now, but all the same she knew he was right. She had never had to do anything in her life. But she didn't want patronage from anyone and, especially, she didn't want patronage from Christian Talbot. 'I've got this far, I'll manage somehow,' she said lamely.

He took a step closer, spreading his legs and propping his arms against the wall. The look in his eyes told her he realized her situation. It told her he knew she was vulnerable. 'You don't have to do it alone,' he said at last, his deep voice somehow quieter.

Her only defence was in the bright, careless smile. 'I'm not alone. I have local council, the Rural Area Society, and lots of friends who'll give me advice if they're asked.'

His lips curled in contempt. 'By "friends" I take it you mean the yuppy lot I've seen hanging around Tregarn House from time to time?'

Again Hannah gave him the bright smile, knowing how much he disliked it. 'The very same.'

Swift, dark fury flashed into his eyes and he finally released her hand. 'Won't you ever learn?' he snapped.

'Not from you, I won't!' she choked, a rush of pride flooding through her. 'Anyway, all I want is my twenty-four acres back, and you'll get your money somehow. Even if it means sweeping the streets from here to Timbuktu.'

She knew she was provoking him far beyond his limits and Hannah held her breath. If he lost control of his temper now there was no saying what he would do. Desperately, she managed a small shrug of indifference but, although she saw his hands tighten with inner rage, he managed to keep a grip on himself.

'Don't push me too far,' he advised quietly. 'Let's stick to the facts and where you will find the extra land if I don't come in with you.'

For a moment they held each other's gaze. Chris's eyes were clear and unfathomable and she wasn't quite certain what lay behind the

33

expression. After a few moments, the familiar cool defiance crept back, her full lips curling in a way she knew made him want to choke her. 'That's my problem,' she said, dismissing the veiled threat implied in his words.

'Your problems are usually other people's. What are you going to do without a shoulder to lean on—without another willing slave?'

'What do you mean, *another* willing slave?'

'Exactly what I said. Isn't that your usual way of getting through life? Finding some poor devil to involve himself in all your empty-headed little schemes? I used to watch you, playing the boys off one by one, and who could blame them for falling for your little tricks? You're a beautiful woman.' He paused, his mouth hardening even more as he added quietly, 'And I haven't forgotten what you did to Mike Jackson.'

For a long moment she stared at him speechlessly. Lord, he knew how to go for the jugular. Why was he torturing her like this? She bit hard into her bottom lip, the blood draining from her cheeks as she returned, 'You must be the most insensitive and arrogant person on this earth.' Her words came out with a steadiness that surprised her and she went on angrily, 'How dare you!'

'I dare because it's the truth. That little affair must have been quite an amusing diversion for you, mustn't it?'

'What—what are you talking about?'

34

'You know damn well what I'm talking about! He was crazy about you and you knew it! And you didn't turn a hair when you threw him over for your brief little escapade into marriage, even though it almost killed him.'

'Threw him over—' Hannah broke in, her tone deliberately freezing. 'I—I didn't. He—he was married to Brenda, I didn't throw him over. I—we didn't have an affair.'

'That's not what I heard. And I don't think I'll ever forgive you for it.'

'Forgive me—' Her words choked in her throat. 'Why should I need your forgiveness?'

'For breaking up his marriage, that's why! Mike was my best pal.'

'I didn't break them up!'

'Then what else did? Mike was no match for you and you knew it, he'd fallen hard and fast and you led him on a merry old dance. I warned him but he wouldn't listen. I know the poor fool almost broke himself trying to please you. When Brenda finally divorced him it was the last straw, he was stony broke—and it was all because of you!' He went on unmercifully, 'And what did you do then . . .?' He paused, unmoved as he watched the angry flush drain from her face, leaving it white. 'You flitted off to Cardiff . . . to your next half-wit . . . and that didn't last two minutes! You left Mike flat . . . devastated. But what would you care about that?'

Mutely Hannah stood her ground, hardly

crediting what she was hearing as the coldness in his voice paralysed her.

Meeting his eyes she saw the glitter of contempt in them and realized grimly that he would never believe a word she said. Lord, he must have been keeping tabs on her for years. That awful time she'd gone through with Chris's friend Mike had happened a long time ago—just before she met Paul—when she'd been eighteen and still wet behind the ears.

Mike must have been lying—boosting his ego! But how could she explain it to Chris Talbot now? Mike was a gambler, surely Talbot knew that? But it was patently clear he would never believe that Mike Jackson's marriage had been over long before she came on the scene, and that, although he'd begged her to go out with him, she never had. Nor had she encouraged him, and certainly had never allowed him to spend money on her! Quite the reverse was true in fact. She knew her father had helped Mike out on several occasions when he'd asked to borrow money.

'It isn't true,' she said expressionlessly at last. 'None of it's true.'

'Isn't it? Well,' Chris's cold voice washed around her, 'that's water under the bridge now and you're in another fix; you need my land. Well, this time, you'll not be allowed to run riot with your crazy schemes. This time, I intend to be involved. And, whether I like your present situation or not, I won't allow you to

36

destroy some other guy like you destroyed my pal.'

'I have no intention of destroying anybody! And it's my land! My father must have made a mistake signing it over to you!'

'No he didn't. He knew what he was doing. And I'm coming in this deal whether you want me in or not. But this time, I'll be calling the shots—and you won't be twisting me around your little finger.'

'I want nothing from you! I *can* and I *will* open Tregarn next summer! I'll show—' She broke off, seeing his stony expression and realizing there was no point in saying any more.

'Not without me, my lovely girl.'

She wheeled to the door. *'Don't call me your lovely girl!'* The ragged fury of her voice startled even herself. She'd heard him call others "lovely girl". It was a careless endearment that meant nothing, yet, for some ridiculous, irrational reason she couldn't stand it. It angered her that he referred to her in the same way as he referred to all his other women.

He caught hold of her wrist, bringing his other hand up to her chin and turning her head to face him. His thumb rubbed against her lower lip, sending an unwanted shiver along her spine. 'I'll call you what I like, *lovely girl*,' he said savagely. 'You need that land but you're not going to get it on your terms.' His glance flicked contemptuously across her face and, after a moment, he let his hand drop. 'Poor Paul . . .' he murmured.

Hannah gulped. 'What—what do you mean . . .*poor* Paul?'

His smile widened but his eyes were like ice. 'Stop playing games, Hannah. You seem to forget that I know you too well—and, I know even more how I make you feel.'

He frightened her. He was too close to the truth. It was useless to deny the obvious. She hadn't known it then, but she did now! She had married Paul loving Chris Talbot. Whatever either of them said now would be a waste of time. The only thing left for her to do now was to end it before it got out of hand.

Her face was pale as she looked up, 'You've just proved to me what I've suspected all along. How dare you talk about my self-centred ways when they don't come anywhere near your smug, egotistical arrogance! I'm not even in the same league! You don't care who you hurt just so long as that conceit of yours is gratified. Well, I don't want you! You can go to—to—'

He eyed her sharply, wry amusement lighting his face. 'You can't even be honest about that, can you? You do want me lovely girl, there's no question about it. And I know with a little persuasion, you'd be more than willing . . . and I certainly am.'

'Well, I'm not!' She could hardly get her

38

breath. She couldn't afford to let him see how much he affected her and she was not going to fall apart now.

There was a long pause as he studied her angry face, then he said quietly, 'This may surprise you, but I'm glad to hear it.'

'Really? How magnanimous of you!'

'When we get together, lovely girl, it won't be because you need my land for a few bungalows. When the time comes it will be because you want to. When you have the guts to admit openly that you have wanted me just as long as I have wanted you.'

His words sent a shiver through her and the image his words provoked flashed through her brain like lightning. 'Don't hold your breath, Talbot!'

She wanted to make him angry but instead he only laughed, stroking the side of his finger along her cheek.

'I've a feeling you're wrong again but, getting back to the matter more immediately to hand, I'll give you time to think things over. I'll come back again tomorrow to see what decision you've arrived at with respect to my becoming senior partner in this fiasco. And I'll also give a little thought on how we can build your bungalows without ripping up the best grazing land for miles.'

'No!' Hannah broke in fiercely, jerking her head away from his touch. 'And you can forget the *"we"*, Talbot! Tregarn is mine! I'll do anything that needs to be done. I can handle it.'

Chris chuckled again. 'You've never handled anything in your life. Don't worry, though, I'll see to things.'

His amused dismissal set her teeth on edge. 'How many times do I have to say this? I don't want *you* to see to things!'

He smiled coldly, turning and walking out of the house, and it was a few moments before Hannah realized he was actually leaving. She watched him climb into his car and start up the engine. Seeing her in the doorway he threw her a grin, waved his hand and drove away, leaving Hannah leaning against the door post, a worried frown etching unmistakably along her brow.

Quietly she closed the door, shutting out the sound of the rain and letting the silence of the house engulf her, an empty reminder of the complications of her life. What a situation! What a mess! But somehow she had to hold on. Somehow she had to get hold of that land and, somehow, she had to hold off Christian Langley Talbot.

Hannah tightened her lips into a grimace. Who had she been fooling all this time? The moment had come for her to be honest with herself at last; to bring out into the open a knowledge that she'd buried deep in her heart for as long as she'd known him. He stirred a deep well-spring of emotion inside her and she just couldn't handle it.

Did she love Christian Langley Talbot? Deep down inside, had she always loved him? Sometimes, when a feeling is so strong, it's very hard to define the difference between love and physical attraction. Whatever it was, she knew she could never ignore it. In her heart she knew how deep-rooted the feeling lay. Probably always had. Probably always would.

Hannah sighed tiredly as she turned off the light and went upstairs.

CHAPTER FOUR

When Hannah came downstairs next morning she was glad to see the sun showing a watery face through the still-threatening clouds. Her head ached and, catching a glimpse of her disconsolate features in the mirror, she found it hard to ignore the dark circles beneath her eyes, indicating a night of restless slumber. The telephone rang as she poured her second cup of tea. Something told her it could be Chris and she didn't want to answer it. But she also knew that if she didn't, he'd keep on ringing until she did, and she certainly wasn't up to that!

On about the tenth ring she walked over to the phone in the hall and muttered a wary

'Hello'.

She waited but the caller didn't answer.

'Hello!' she called again, this time a little louder but again there was no reply. 'Who is this? Hello! Hello!'

Hannah was suddenly shaking. She could hear the caller's quickened breath in her ear, almost as though he were standing next to her. *'Who is this? Why don't you answer?'*

She replaced the receiver with a jerk, a sick feeling clawing at her heart. She could *never* put up with this! She had more than enough worries to cope with without weird phone calls adding to them. Hannah sat down wearily on the telephone seat, shivering a little and her hands coming up to her face. Her fingertips rubbed along her forehead and she glanced at her reflection again. It was ridiculous to think that this could be the same lunatic she'd encountered on the road but, somehow, instinct told her it was. Why couldn't he leave her alone? It was ludicrous! Ludicrous and fearful!

After a few minutes Hannah walked to the door and opened it. Her whole life seemed to be tumbling upside down and there didn't seem to be much she could do about it!

'Oh, Tregarn, Tregarn, thank goodness I still have you.'

She closed her eyes for a moment, her nostrils picking up the sweet scents of the morning. The sun was like a welcome friend, warm and friendly against her face and standing there, she was suddenly filled with an odd kind of peacefulness—a great and wonderful peacefulness.

The fields all around dipped away towards the river in waves of rippling green and gold, and a gentle breeze brushed her cheeks. For one brief moment things so mundane as nuisance calls, mad drivers—not to mention a prickly, far-too-attractive neighbour—became no more than the blurred trivia of life. She still had Tregarn!

Tregarn was all that mattered now. Her heart began to swell with a kind of love; an emotion she had never known existed and it was bringing a strange feeling of sadness. Did the sadness come from knowing that this was a love she had never known before? Never appreciated before?

Her eyes blurred as she looked out over the crested hills and her throat grew tight with sudden tears.

Suddenly, she found she was crying now in great racking sobs and yet she could not put into words the exact reason why. Chris Talbot was part of it. Tregarn, Paul, her parents too. And she knew that until today she had not known quite how little value she had placed on this land, and how much she truly loved it.

She tore herself away from her sadness and ran back into the kitchen, dashing off what remained of her now cold tea. The best thing to do in times like this she told herself was to keep busy. And she could certainly do that! There was plenty to do.

The young magnolia saplings and azalea shrubs had been delivered yesterday and setting them out for Mr Wilkinson to plant would be enough work for her to do to last the whole of the day.

Hannah stacked a few breakfast dishes in the machine and fed the cats. Handling a hundred or so young magnolia trees alone would be hard and heavy work but she didn't care. It was work that would tire her out and that thought pleased her. It pleased her because, when bedtime came round again, she would be too tired to think or care about anything other than Tregarn.

When Hannah went outside a little while later she felt again that intangible something stir inside her. She stood for some minutes looking round at the acres of land her parents had left in her care. Away to her left lay the wooded south-west, silent and serene, and beyond that, shimmered the blue haze of the Black Mountains, docile and distant on the still, morning air.

She would make this project pay! She had to! She would take up the challenge no matter what. After all, if Scarlett O'Hara could do it, so could she! Except, she thought ruefully, Christian Langley Talbot was certainly no Rhett Butler!

Suddenly, she felt supremely independent! And it was a warm, exciting feeling because, to make this place pay, would be the first worthwhile thing she had ever done in her life.

She loaded the wheelbarrow and, in a little over two hours, already a good quarter of the shrubs had been transferred from the hothouse to the half-acre marked out for them around the gothic arches of the walled garden. Already her arms and her back had begun to ache but it didn't matter. Hannah was enjoying herself even though the twenty-four labours of Hercules could not have been more strenuous or more exhausting.

*   *   *

'*Hannah.*'

Someone was calling her name and, wiping her wrist along her forehead, she looked up to see the man approach, and even from that distance she felt herself stiffen as she recognized Chris Talbot's familiar shape closing the Shogun door. She turned back quickly to the wheelbarrow, lifting the handles and, staggering a little with the weight, pushed it crookedly further along the path.

He strolled towards her. 'Are you some sort of masochist?' was his gruff comment. 'Couldn't you leave that sort of job for Wilkinson?'

'I enjoy gardening.' Hannah kept her eyes

45

straight ahead, concentrating on her task.

'Gardening?' he repeated with a soft laugh. 'I'd hardly call it that! You'll have shoulders like Frank Bruno shoving that thing around all day. And just look at your legs—have you no sense at all?'

She glanced down quickly, noticing the red weals where the branches of the magnolias had caught them—some of them deep enough to bring blood to the surface—and she wished she'd had the sense to wear her jeans instead of the brief cut-off shorts.

'Let me have it,' he rasped, reaching for the wheelbarrow and pushing it easily along the path. 'If your father could see you now he'd have you certified.'

Hannah's expression hardened. 'You underestimate me—and my father! My dad taught me more about running this place than you know. This has to be done and I'm doing it!'

'No you're not—you'll kill yourself.'

His flat observation made her stop, her head tilting up and the gleam in her eye a bright challenge. 'And you're going to stop me, I suppose?' she asked tonelessly. 'What are you doing here, anyway? Have you come to your senses and decided to sell back my acres?'

Chris put down the wheelbarrow and turned slowly back to face her. 'It's taken me a while to find you. When you didn't answer the door, I thought perhaps you'd gone into Tregarn

46

town. Then, on the way back to Twr Gwyn, one of my men said he thought he'd seen you carrying half of Sherwood Forest from that monster of a greenhouse.'

'That monster of a greenhouse cost me an arm and a leg I'll have you know. And it's a *hothouse*!'

'What do you want a hothouse for?'

Hannah sighed inwardly. 'For when we get the tropical stuff.'

'I thought this was supposed to be a holiday centre, not Kew Gardens.'

'Look, Talbot, I haven't time to stand here listening to your inane jokes. I want to get these shrubs to the walled garden ready for planting on Monday.'

'What's the matter with your eyes?'

'What?' She turned her head away, shading her eyes. 'Nothing's the matter with them.'

'Look at me.'

His hand went to her chin, tilting it. 'They're all red; have you been crying?' His voice was rough.

She couldn't turn away from him now, and for some reason she didn't even try. Her eyes, blue, luminous and big were upturned, holding his, and edging the long dark lashes were the red, tell-tale signs of tears.

'Why have you been crying? What's wrong now?'

His question was asked brusquely, impatiently. Yet, was she imagining it, or was

47

there a kind of gentleness softening his tone? She doubted it but, nevertheless, his manner made her throat grow even tighter. If she said something now she knew she would cry again so, biting hard on her bottom lip, she shook her head.

His hands were still on her face, his fingers buried in the long swathe of her dark hair. 'Has something else happened to upset you this morning?'

Again she shook her head.

'Then what's the matter?'

He took a step closer, his body within touching distance of hers and she pulled herself together with a start. She mustn't allow herself to feel this way!

'Chris, don't!' She started to shake a little. They were standing so close he must have felt her tremor, and she wondered too if he could feel the uneven bumping of her heart.

'Why are you shaking?' he interrupted, ignoring her plea. 'Are you cold?'

Hannah shook her head. 'No, I'm not cold.'

'Then why are you shaking so much?'

She straightened her shoulders. 'I'm—I'm fine!' she stammered. 'It's all this work I suppose. Pushing a barrow up and down for two hours is not my usual occupation and I'm not used to it. It's only muscle tension—I'll get the hang of it given time.' And, as he continued to look at her, she managed a brightness she was far from feeling. 'I know

48

what you're thinking and you're dead wrong! Your imagination's working overtime as usual. I'm not trembling with passion if that's what you're hoping I'll say.'

His face hardened. 'Far from it I should think.' Then his look took on a sudden harshness. 'Come on, let's go. I'll send some of my men to bring the rest of these shrubs down.'

She swallowed hard. 'No! Tregarn is my responsibility! I don't want your men doing my work! Besides, I can manage if I'm left alone.'

'I said let's go.' He took her arm and even though she struggled against him she couldn't free herself from his long, strong fingers. He led her back along the path and towards the house, reaching it without a word, pushing open the back door and propelling her in. 'Even Percy Thrower took a break now and then. Besides, we have things to discuss.'

'Not again.'

'Yes . . . again.'

Hannah closed the door behind them, having no alternative but to do as he said. She had hoped she wouldn't see him again today, but that had been a fragile hope. All she really wanted to do was to be left alone to sort herself out, but it clearly wasn't to be.

'How about some coffee?' he asked as she opened the kitchen door, ducking her head under his arm as he leaned it against the frame.

Hannah shrugged, 'Why not?'

Hannah walked slowly into the kitchen. And, as she switched on the coffee-maker she was conscious of Chris Talbot as he strolled over to the window, looking out.

Suddenly, the phone rang again and Hannah froze. She jerked her head towards it, willing it to stop and praying it was not the nuisance caller again.

'Well? Aren't you going to answer it?'

'Yes, of course.' Hannah gathered herself and moved jerkily to the phone, but, as she reached to pick up the receiver on the hall table, it stopped again. She looked back quickly at Chris Talbot, relief bright in her eyes. 'Probably a wrong number.'

He moved back to the table as she poured the coffee into two mugs. 'Good Lord, woman, just look at you,' he murmured, 'and look at these . . .' reaching out and gently patting at her smarting thighs. 'What a mess.'

Hannah drew away. 'They're just scratches. Nothing that a little Savlon won't cure.'

'What were you doing to get your legs in this state?' he asked, steering her firmly towards the sink and turning on the tap. 'Rolling about on a bed of thorns?'

He tore off a couple of strips of kitchen roll and moistened them under the tap then, gently, he cleansed her cuts, dabbing around the swollen weals with the touch of a Harley Street surgeon.

Hannah stood motionless, keeping her head bowed. He was warm and strong against her, his hands, while he cleansed her, were as gentle as a mother's with a child. That gentleness shook her, disturbed her senses, and she was forced to keep her head low to stop herself from falling against him, to feel his arms come around her and hold her close.

She held her breath. This apparent solicitude was a side of Chris Talbot that she had never seen before—never known existed—and its effect upon her was devastating.

He turned off the tap with his right elbow, bringing his left hand up along her back. His hand was wet. Hannah felt the dampness seeping through her thin cotton shirt at her back. Everything about him was masculine, and also, everything about him was a magnet—a come-on!

'I should kiss you better,' he smiled easily, his voice low and daring her to let him.

'No . . . you shouldn't.' Hannah shook her head, keeping it low, and Chris didn't push her, although she knew that if he had she would have been unable to resist him. Instead he dried her with the towel and made her sit back at the table, bending on one knee and smoothing on some antiseptic cream he found in the bathroom cabinet.

'Well, what have we to discuss this morning?' she asked dully, when he'd finished his ministrations. 'Have you come with another of your bright ideas?'

His mouth tightened as he straightened up, sitting down and resting his ankle across the knee of his other leg. 'I didn't spend all morning looking for you just to start another fight.'

'Well, that's something to be thankful for at least.'

'And contrary to your imaginings, I do have other things to think about apart from sorting out your pathetic affairs.'

Hannah's eyes glittered her distaste. 'I find that hard to believe.'

Chris laughed tauntingly. 'You flatter yourself, lovely girl. I've seen what happens to guys who walk into your pretty little web and there's no way I'm going to be one of them unless it's on my terms.' His eyes narrowed a fraction. 'What I want to discuss is purely business and how best we can make Tregarn earn its keep.'

Hannah's eyes flashed blue fire. '*We?*'

'Yes, we,' he confirmed evenly. 'And try to be sensible for once in your life. I've had an idea that would work equally well for both of us.'

'You seem to keep forgetting, there are three of us—there's the bank to consider. And I hope this new idea's an improvement on your last one.'

It gratified her that he looked

uncomfortable. 'I think so. By the way, have you managed to speak to your absent partner yet?'

'No. There's no need,' Hannah replied tersely. 'Paul has nothing to do with Tregarn now.' Her mouth felt dry. 'All decisions will be mine.'

'Very sensible. And you'll be pleased to know, I've come up with an alternative to those twenty-four acres.'

Hannah watched his expression, wondering what was to come now. Brown eyes scrutinized her, studying her face with grim attention before he went on, 'Instead of using that land we'll extend the main house. My investment will finance another, say, ten or twelve guest rooms to be build on the back.'

'On the—'

'Let me finish,' he went on coolly. 'They needn't be expensive, just basic, with a shower unit perhaps, and the guests can eat in the house—in the main dining-room.' He sat back, his dark eyes studying her reaction in half amusement. 'Well, what do you think?'

Hannah gasped. It was a splendid idea. Yet, even through the swell of astonishment she had the wit to realize it wasn't a bad deal for him, either. The land by the lake was good land, flat and firm for training and rich for pasture. He'd clearly rather throw a good deal of money into the project than give those acres up and, deep down, she had to admit the sense

53

of his proposal.

He waited, still watching. 'Well?'

'I'd—need to think about it,' she whispered numbly. 'It sounds . . . reasonable. But—but—what about the tennis courts?'

His face hardened into a look of perplexity. 'Tennis courts. What about the tennis courts?'

'They're already being laid at the back of the house. Where else could we put them when—?' She broke off, suddenly aware she, too, was already talking in terms of "we".

He sighed in annoyance, his smile mocking. 'I'm sure we'd find somewhere for them. Surely, the accommodation is the main priority?'

'I suppose so,' she mumbled, her mouth feeling even more dry.

'There's one condition.'

'Ahh . . .!' Hannah's contempt expressed itself in one syllable. 'Of course, there had to be a condition,' she conceded bitterly.

His mouth twisted wryly, anticipating her thoughts. 'If you're thinking what I think you're thinking, you're well off course, lovely girl,' he gritted. 'My condition is not that, tempting as it is. My condition is that my men do the work—I'll even get some contractors in if necessary, that way we'll save money.'

Hannah's mouth dropped in astonishment. 'But surely your men won't agree to that?'

'You've lived too long in Yuppieland,' he came back scathingly, throwing her a look that

54

was cold and empty. 'You've forgotten our country code. We still help each other around here, or have you forgotten?'

'You surely can't mean that?'

'I do, and that's the condition. Take it or leave it. If Tregarn is to become profitable again time is of the essence and, with a bit of good luck, it could be done inside a year. Besides, I liked your father, he was a good man—a good friend and neighbour. He helped my father once years ago and I owe him. I'm doing this for him as much as anything, certainly not for his spoiled brat of a daughter.'

'That's a terrible thing to say.'

Chris regarded her with the old familiar look of dislike. 'The truth hurts, doesn't it? If your father hadn't been so intent on giving you the life he thought you deserved—a useless life that just hummed along in the way you wanted it—he'd have had no need to sell the Rhysnant land to me in the first place.'

'*What?*'

'Oh, come on. How else could he have paid for your expensive trips abroad with your jet-setting friends . . . or your winter skiing . . . or the Caribbean cruises, etcetera, etcetera?'

Hannah's face had been pale before but now it was deathly white. 'What are you saying?' The question came little more than a whisper.

Chris's face hardened. 'Don't play the

innocent with me. How much do you think it takes to run a place like this? You must have known your father had been trying to keep his head above water for over a year. You must have known how much this project meant to him! And how he'd been trying to get it off the ground! And yet, in spite of that, you always came along with your selfish ideas, like the time you got married and you just had to go to the West Indies for your honeymoon. How could anyone with any feeling do that? It must have been the last straw for him.'

Hannah shrank away. She remembered the Barbados trip clearly. She hadn't wanted to go but Paul had insisted. She hadn't known until it was too late that Paul had borrowed the money from her father and, when she offered to repay it, her Dad had declined. He'd said the holiday was to be his wedding present. And he'd been so insistent on paying for it that in the end she'd agreed, but only because it seemed to make him happy.

'You're wrong! I didn't—'

His voice was crisp with contempt and distaste as he finished. 'Don't you ever think of anyone but yourself?'

Hannah tossed her head in defiance. 'Of course, but I don't expect you to believe a word I say!'

His eyes glinted. 'Why should I believe you?'

'Because it would be the truth! Because—'

She broke off with a sob, her throat raw now with suppressed tears and her head throbbing.

Chris glanced quickly at her pale, set face. 'You're not putting up a bad little show. You've almost got me believing it.'

Hannah jerked her arm away, lifting her head defiantly again. 'It's the truth!'

His hand came across to rest on her arm again. 'All right, calm down, no need to get so worked up.' His mouth was set in a firm line but now his eyes were betraying an unexpected understanding, as if seeing a side of her that he hadn't known existed and, with the realization, came a softening of his tone.

'Look, I'm sorry if I've misjudged you. Perhaps your dad did keep his problems away from you after all, and I'm prepared to take back most of what I said. But at least admit now that you need someone to help you— especially me. You'll never make it on your own.'

'Don't flatter yourself!' She got to her feet quickly, hot tears were gathering behind her eyes. For a moment she swayed against the table and, as he stood up too, Chris's arms came round her in support. She pulled free, blinking back the tears and stubbornly refusing his arms of comfort. 'I—I—'

She broke off, curling her nails into her palms. What could she say? How could she explain? No matter what she said he'd never believe her. Words were nothing. To him she

57

would always be the spoilt darling he believed her to be.

Chris's voice, cutting through her thoughts, was quiet and still and held a strangely puzzled tone. 'I thought you knew how tough things were at Tregarn.'

Hannah threw him an incredulous look and turned away. 'I didn't know,' she murmured.

There was a long pause as Chris studied her. Uncomfortable under his dark assessing gaze, Hannah, with trembling hands, picked up the mugs and took them over to the sink to rinse them. When she turned back to face him, drying her hands on the towel, he was still studying her grimly.

'Will you agree to my idea?' he asked quietly, at last.

Hannah sighed in resignation. 'I can't see that I have a choice.'

'No, you haven't.' He paused again, adding briskly a moment later, as though suddenly coming to a decision. 'I'll get all the necessary wheels in motion tomorrow. Your father already had planning permission, didn't he?' At Hannah's brief nod he continued, 'Right, I'll come over in the morning and bring a team of my men to start work.' He gave her a fleeting, one-sided smile. 'It's a tall order looking at the state of this place. But the sooner we get moving the sooner it'll be finished.'

Hannah held his gaze, her chin high and

proud and her blue eyes remote. She imagined an odd note of derision in his voice again but as she looked up his expression gave nothing away. 'Very well,' she agreed finally. 'But we must make sure all this is done on a sound business footing, neither of us must lose out.'

'Oh, we won't,' he replied, dark eyes narrowing. 'I've already told you I believe in getting value on my investments.'

Hannah's smile was touched with bitterness. 'Indeed you have.'

He shrugged indifferently, spreading his hands. 'Now that's settled, how about some more coffee? Then I must go, I have work to do.'

Totally nonplussed, Hannah picked up his mug from the draining board and refilled it. She was feeling a little calmer now, but still confused. She wanted to ask him why he was prepared to help her out like this when he despised her so much. Perhaps it amused his male ego that he was the only one in a position to help out an old enemy—one who had spent her life looking at him from over her nose.

She wanted desperately to counter-attack. She felt she needed to justify her privileged background, and also to prove to him that she wasn't the spineless wonder he evidently believed her to be. Questions formed in her head but before she could ask them she heard him saying casually, 'Be ready to look over some papers tomorrow.'

She spun round quickly. 'But it's Sunday tomorrow.'

'My solicitor won't bother about that, just be ready.'

'Does everybody jump when you snap your fingers?' she gritted, smarting again at his air of cocksureness.

'Usually.'

Straightening her shoulders she acquiesced with a deep sigh, 'Very well, I'll be ready.'

She moved away from him to the window seat but Chris, mug in hand, came to sit beside her. She edged away as she felt his warmth touching her again.

'Why are you involving yourself in this?' she asked directly. 'Why are you doing this for Tregarn?'

He paused, sipping at his coffee and then putting it down on the arm of the seat. 'Because Tregarn has always had potential,' he murmured after a long pause. 'And because I can't see you making a go of it on your own.' He anticipated her hasty interruption. 'Besides, I have enough men around Twr Gwyn who will be only too willing to give a hand—if only for your old man's sake.' He smiled at her aloof expression. 'I know you don't like it, but you'll have to come round to it in the end so you might just as well get used to it—I'm taking over. Anyway, it's for my benefit as much as yours.' He laughed shortly. 'Does that answer your question, lovely girl?

60

His eyes were bright now—teasing. With a brief nod of his blond head, he stood up, picking up the mug and placing it back on the table. Striding to the door he turned briefly, sizing up Hannah's stricken face as she followed him, and sweeping over the trim shape in the blue cut-off jeans and cotton shirt. 'Better give those cuts another bathe tonight,' he suggested, 'they look pretty sore to me.' He tilted her downcast face upwards. 'And if you play your cards right . . . if you dress yourself to look more like a girl than a brickie's labourer—I might even treat you to lunch.'

CHAPTER FIVE

The next morning Hannah overslept. She awoke feeling tense and glanced impatiently at the clock on the bedside table and, mindful of the fact that Chris Talbot had said he was coming round again today to take her to meet his solicitor, she got up quickly and took a shower.

As the water flowed over her she thought again of Chris Talbot's solution to her problems. Was it possible, as he'd admitted, that he was helping her for her father's sake, paying off a few long-standing favours? Or was it that he too could see Tregarn as a way of adding a few more pounds to his already swollen bank account, and without giving up his twenty-four newly acquired, valuable acres?

Or perhaps there was something more! And if there was, what was it? What was he up to? What did he want?

She sighed deeply, angry with herself that she might have miscalculated his humiliating honesty. Perhaps after all, he was only being a friendly, caring neighbour as he'd suggested.

Hannah shook her dark wet hair, the movement sending sprinklets of water across the glass of the shower cabinet. Somehow she didn't think it was only that. He *must* have something else in mind.

Hannah stepped out, wrapping herself in a towel as she padded along to her bedroom. Taking her favourite suit from the wardrobe she slipped it on, telling herself she should take this offer purely as it stood. The idea of extending the main building was quite obvious, and she couldn't think why she hadn't thought of it before. But, all the same, somewhere deep inside a persistent little voice kept on telling her to be on her guard.

A little after eight o'clock Hannah heard the sound of vans and cars milling around in the drive. In all, eleven of Chris's men had been 'volunteered' and Hannah's first job, after she had shown the foreman where everything was stored, was to make coffee for them all.

Chris arrived a little after nine. His mud-spattered Shogun was replaced this morning by a dark-grey Mercedes, and as Hannah looked out at it from the window she fumed inwardly, its sleek elegance reminding her of the many hopeful females who must have experienced the self-indulgence of its owner on the luxurious, leather-upholstered comfort of its wide back seat.

When she opened the door Chris's dark eyes swept over her in open approval. 'That's better,' he murmured, smilingly.

Hannah moved to let him in, glad she had deliberately chosen one of her favourite—and most expensive—suits, determined to look as she'd always looked—or at least hoped she'd looked—sensuously assured.

The suit was a pale yellow silk fastened only by two small buttons at the waist and, although it seemed at first glance she was wearing nothing underneath, it did in fact cover a matching camisole. Rimless tinted glasses shielded her eyes and her hair was sleeked back into a demure twist. Two final touches— one, a moss agate pinned to her lapel and the second, a touch of expensively subtle perfume dabbed behind her ears—and the confident image she was determined to maintain was achieved.

Brickie's labourer indeed!

She smiled a little stiffly as Chris stepped past her into the hallway, knowing his nostrils had caught the fragrance of her perfume. His working jeans and open-necked shirt had been discarded this morning for a suit. The cut of it emphasized the broadness of his shoulders, heightening his masculinity instead of restraining it. It crossed her mind she had never seen a man as attractive as Chris Talbot—especially first thing on a Sunday morning!

'I thought you were sending your men to help me out, not to take over completely,' she murmured as they stood together in the doorway.

He grinned, his teeth showing white and even in the morning sun. 'They're my heavy bunch, they'll do all the rough stuff.'

'And what have you in mind for me?'

His grin widened as he returned smoothly, 'What do you suggest?'

Hannah chose to ignore his obvious innuendo and held his gaze boldly. 'But there must be *something* I can do. After all, it's still my place,' she reminded him. 'Either I do my share or the deal's off.'

'Don't worry, there'll be lots for you to do later on,' he answered non-committally. 'I'm sure I'll think of something.'

'Please do.' She didn't even bother to hide the edge of sarcasm. 'After all, now that you've put yourself in charge, perhaps you'll inform me when I can do whatever you consider suitable for my delicate hands—like watering

64

the shrubbery for example, or dusting the roses.'

'Of course.' Chris stood leaning backwards against the door, amused dark eyes surveying her flushed face. 'But that won't be for some time yet. There's plenty of heavy work to do around here before we can even consider letting you loose on the roses. Once they've got rid of the deadwood we'll start on the project proper. Which reminds me . . . have you kept the sketches and estimates your father had drawn up?'

'Yes, they're all here.'

'Good. Galbraith, my solicitor, is doing me a great favour by seeing us today.'

Hannah shrugged slightly. 'You don't waste time, do you?'

'Never,' he murmured, unperturbed by her mockery, then giving her a disarming smile, he ordered, 'I'll take those.'

Hannah handed him the bulging packet and, as they went outside to the car, he opened the door and she climbed in.

She saw how his eyes slid to the length of her leg, exposed by the movement of her skirt. Settling in her seat she restored her skirt to its proper position and crossed her legs, throwing him a questioning glance as he continued to stand by the open door. 'Is something wrong?'

'No, not a thing.'

He closed the door and walked round the car, settling himself behind the wheel. He drove the car out of the drive and on to the main Cardiff road. Once there, Chris slipped up a gear and they set off on the forty-five minute journey into the city.

They didn't say much. Fifteen minutes must have passed before she finally made the wry comment, 'I don't believe I've ever had the pleasure of driving into Cardiff with you before—and in such style, too.'

Chris grunted. 'I suppose that's a hint about my Merc? Personally, I prefer a horse any time but image counts these days, and this is all part of my image.'

'I see.' Hannah glanced at his good-looking profile. 'So this posh car's merely to keep up your image? Deep down you're just a country boy?'

She saw his mouth quirk into a wry smile. 'I suppose so. Although, as I've already told you, horses are much more to my taste.' He turned to glance at her briefly, his expression sarcastic. 'But they were never yours, were they?'

'No,' she murmured, leaning her head back.

Actually, although she didn't correct him, he was quite wrong about that. When she'd been small and very young there'd been nothing more thrilling for her than to ride out across the valleys. Her father had despaired of her many times, often joking that the hospital must have made a mistake on the morning she was born, and she really should have been a

66

boy.

How she'd adored her round-bellied little pony, Midnight and, later on, as she'd grown a little older, her horse, Bobby. She smiled to herself, remembering. There had been many a night when she'd preferred sharing their stable to her soft comfortable bed, especially on cold winter nights. Her father had often come to look for her, always finding her curled up in the warm, sweet-smelling straw. He'd never tried to stop her, leaving her where she was and covering her with a blanket, leaving her to her dreams.

But, of course, that was in the days when the teenaged Chris Talbot had been away at college so he couldn't have known her very much then. By the time they met she was already at finishing school in France and saw him only infrequently during her visits home, her image as a snooty young featherbrain already well and truly moulded.

She began to wonder if things would have been different if she'd met Chris Talbot when she'd been older. Would there still have been this antagonism between them? She pursed her lips and watched the countryside fly past.

Yes, she thought wryly, she supposed there would. There had never been any love lost between them.

St Peter's clock was striking noon as they came out of Henry Galbraith's office in St Andrew's Square. The solicitor would send a

67

surveyor along to check Chris's plans for the annexe, the necessary papers would be drawn up, and the guests' accommodation area would be increased by a substantial amount while her home, her privacy at Tregarn, would shrink.

But, she conceded, she could make a decent flat out of the attics and she was grateful that a solution had been found. At least now she had some elbow-room.

Chris's hand curled around her elbow as they walked out to the car. 'I did promise lunch remember? That didn't take too long, we've got bags of time. Let's find a pub or something and grab a bite to eat. I'm hungry, how about you?'

Hannah murmured her agreement and fumbled in her bag for her sun-glasses, 'Lunch sounds fine.'

They strolled along St Mary Street and turned into one of the pretty, glass-roofed arcades that meander pleasantly through to Cardiff's other main thoroughfare. Queen Street. They found a small Italian restaurant and, once inside, they were led across to a table for two by the window.

They sat down and, as Chris scanned the menu, Hannah broke open one of the warm rolls and took a pat of butter. It all seemed so normal, so ordinary, sitting with him like this and, taking a bite of the roll, she looked around. It surprised her how many people knew them and, as she smiled and nodded her recognition at two or three couples sitting nearby, she noted the way they were being watched.

Hannah grimaced inwardly. 'I wonder if my name will be added to their list.'

Chris looked up. 'List? What list?'

'Your list of accomplishments.'

'What are you talking about?'

'Look around. Look at their faces. We're both pretty well known around here and isn't it a fact that any woman seen with you is automatically assumed to be your latest playmate? I suppose they're wondering why it took so long for you to get round to me.'

He frowned in annoyance. 'That's an exaggeration, I'm afraid.'

'Is it?'

'Most certainly it is in this case.'

'Most *definitely* it is in this case!'

Chris laid the menu aside, looking across and holding her gaze. 'Shall we call a truce over lunch? Trying to keep up with your sharp little barbs is already giving me indigestion. Besides—' He grinned, his eyes sliding downwards over the silk suit as it wrapped around her so modestly; its soft folds showing every subtle curve of her shape—'you're far too attractive a lunch date for me to waste time cutting you down to size.'

Hannah glanced at him and in spite of everything, smiled back. He was very sure of himself. But then, why shouldn't he be?

Women never refused him, and it was hard to blame them. He projected such an overwhelming virility that even just to sit with him like this was as seductive as the most expert technique.

He was still speaking, 'Which brings me to something else that may cause a few waves.'

'Oh? And that is . . .?'

'Tregarn's going to be pretty uncomfortable for a week or two so I think you'd better move into my place.'

The colour left her face, draining from her cheeks until they were as pale as ivory. For a moment his words failed to make sense, unconnected in her mind like pieces of a puzzle. '*What?*'

'I said, I think you'd be better staying at Twr Gwyn until the dust settles.'

She felt her stomach tighten. 'I *knew* it!' she snapped angrily. 'I knew all the time that you were manoeuvring to get me to move in with you! Well, you can forget it! You really take the biscuit Chris Talbot! There are limits to everything and you've just reached mine!'

Panic and fury were now taking the place of shock. Even as he sat there—so near she could reach out and touch him—he seemed to loom. He was too close! His presence was making her feel insignificant as always, confusing her, overwhelming her senses. 'You can go to blazes with your offer of accommodation, I'll manage quite well at Tregarn! Why I'd—I'd

70

rather move in with a . . . a . . . *gerbil* than move in with you! I know what you have in mind!'

He picked up his glass and filled it with water, dropping several ice cubes into it. Lifting it to his lips he took a sip, his eyes not once leaving her face. Hannah watched his muscular throat working as he drank. Swiftly, she looked away again, cursing the physical response he sparked off in her.

Chris put his glass down and asked quietly, 'Did I suggest something improper?'

'Oh, I'm sorry,' she grated bitterly. 'Don't tell me I've got hold of the wrong end of the stick again.'

His gaze moved over her. Irritation, mingled with pure sexual speculation, was in his eyes—as if his mind was already well ahead of her. It was a look that said any woman would be satisfied in his arms.

When he spoke his voice was harsh with impatience. 'I'll be honest enough to admit I wouldn't say no, even though you're such a pain in the—' He broke off, taking a sip of water then putting the glass down. 'A man would be a fool to refuse such a tempting offer if it was made. But, yes, this time you have misunderstood me. You have no need to worry because, for once in my life, sex has nothing to do with it.'

Her eyes flashed suspiciously, 'No? Then why do you want me at Twr Gwyn?'

'Simply because it will become messy at

71

Tregarn and I think you'll be more comfortable at my place.'

Hannah tried desperately to think of something else to say, but, thankfully the waiter came along just then to take their order and they let the subject drop until they were drinking their coffee.

Watching him covertly, Hannah pushed her spoon around the thick creamy froth and murmured, 'Are you serious when you say you only want me to stay at your place because of the state of Tregarn?'

'Yes, I am. It could get very dangerous when we start to tear it apart, I wouldn't want you to get hurt.'

Her eyes narrowed. 'I find it hard to believe that your only concern is about my safety, especially knowing your reputation. You must think me as green as grass. No wonder you've never married if you think women can't read you like a book.'

'You're wrong again,' he said sharply. 'I *have* been married.'

His words stunned her. She'd never associated Chris Talbot with a wife and a sudden unreasoning jealousy swept over her. A terrible rage surged as she thought of this woman who had the right to wait for him to come home to her at night. To come home and love her. A faceless woman who had more right than anyone else to touch him.

'Who . . . who is . . . she? When—when . . ?'

she stammered.

His voice was flat when he spoke again and his eyes filled with contempt. 'It was a long time ago.'

'Any children?'

'No.'

Hannah felt cold. 'Why all the secrecy?' she whispered. 'Surely, after knowing you all my life I would have heard *something* about it.'

He gave a slight shrug. 'It was no secret, but let's drop it.'

'Where is she now?'

'I said, let's drop it. We're divorced and that's the end of it.'

His cold manner warned her not to ask any more questions and she sat back in her chair, all the breath taken out of her. It was beyond her how she had not heard any of this. And, as the knowledge sank in, it was even more beyond her that any woman who had been Chris's wife could leave him. Whoever she was, she must have been very special.

She saw him watching her, studying her reaction. And there was a sadness behind his eyes that made her heart jolt sickeningly. He didn't .smile, but he said softly, almost indifferently, 'Sorry . . . I didn't mean to give you such a shock, I thought you knew.'

Hannah shook her head. 'No, I didn't know.'

'It wasn't anyone you know. It was a girl I met in Ireland, and it's a part of my life that I

73

prefer not to talk about.' He picked up his glass of water and took another sip, setting it down again before he spoke again. 'I'm telling you this so that you'll understand how I feel about marriage. It may be old hat these days, but I for one have always taken it seriously. When she left me it hurt like blazes and I tried to shut away all traces of her.'

'What was her name?'

'Joyce.'

'You sound angry, as though you disliked her.'

'Do I?' He shook his head. 'I liked her well enough, and, on reflection when all the dust cleared away. I can only blame myself for what happened between us. Now, I'd rather forget about it.'

'That's not always so easy.'

Chris shrugged slightly, 'Perhaps not. But it hurt like hell when she went . . , a bruised ego, I suppose.' He glanced across, throwing her a brief smile that reminded her of a little boy. 'It was a nasty business. Joyce felt betrayed and as a result we became just two more statistics in the divorce court,' he went on bitterly. 'No one can live with betrayal.'

'No . . . that must be the worst way of all to end a marriage. These days it can be quite civilized—by mutual consent when things— when things—' She trailed off miserably.

Chris's eyes narrowed as he eyed her broodingly. 'Is that how you and Paul ended

74

yours?'

Hannah bit her bottom lip guiltily. He believed her to be so shallow—so starry-eyed. She hadn't meant to raise unhappy memories for him, but she resented terribly the way he looked on her as nothing more than a pretty, useless butterfly without a vestige of real feeling. 'I'm sorry,' she murmured. 'I only meant to say that sometimes divorce is what both parties want. It—it must have been very painful for you.'

His eyes challenged her. 'Ah yes, you know all about that kind of pain, don't you?' he said brutally.

Stung, she took a steadying breath, focusing coldly on him and uttering without emotion, 'You don't know me at all.'

He laughed grimly, breaking the tense silence. 'Perhaps not,' he admitted. 'But your track record tells me otherwise. Anyway, it took me quite a while to accustom myself to the fact that anyone could leave me. After all, I wouldn't deliberately set out to hurt anyone—I'm a fairly ordinary sort of man.'

Ordinary! She gazed at him, saying nothing, but thinking how wrong he was. Her thoughts went back to Paul and wondered why he had never affected her so potently as Chris Talbot always had. Why no other man affected her this way.

'But don't worry, I'll be a model of propriety when you come to Twr Gwyn,' he added with a

75

grin. 'It's purely a business arrangement. I won't come anywhere near you.' He reached for her hand. 'Unless, of course, you twist my arm.'

Hannah flushed, wrenching her hand away but saying nothing.

CHAPTER SIX

Hannah woke early next morning. Morosely, she got up and threw on a robe, her bare feet padding along the passage to the 'glory hole' to unearth the pair of old-fashioned suitcases. She did as Chris told her and threw a few of her things into one of them, absorbed in the tumult of her thoughts and the feeling that her cosy, untroubled world had been thrown completely off course. Then she showered and washed her hair, slipping the robe back on as she made her way downstairs into the kitchen.

She ground more beans and made fresh coffee, lolling her damp head against the cupboard door and watching the dark brew drip through the filter, frowning a little as unbidden and unwelcome thoughts of Chris crept back into her mind.

A little before 8.30, the sound of cars in the drive sent Hannah's glance darting to the window. Was it Chris? If it was, he was early, she hadn't expected him so soon. He'd said nine o'clock, but that could mean anything between ten or eleven with so much to do at Twr Gwyn. Even so, the window glass reflected her disappointment when she found that it wasn't.

Two pick-up trucks turned into the drive and a couple of men got out. She recognized them as two who had been here yesterday, one of them spotting her through the open window and giving her a wave. Hannah waved back, reverting her attention to the dripping of the coffee and, when it had finished, she filled a mug and wrapped her cold hands around it.

It could only be her nerves making her feel so cold, the morning was already far too warm for comfort.

The day was even hotter by the time Chris arrived. His blond-streaked hair was tousled and his jaw darkened by the overnight growth of beard and, as she watched him stride towards the house, he reminded Hannah of a Viking. Quickly, she stood up, tossing another round of bread into the toaster and concentrating her thoughts on other things.

A few minutes later she heard his knock and the door opened. Hannah turned to greet him and, suddenly, he was standing in front of her, measuring her with that now-familiar, searching gaze.

She poured him a cup. 'Black, and one sugar as I remember.'

Chris shrugged, apparently finding the sight

of her lightly clad body of far greater interest than any cup of coffee. He muttered his thanks and took the cup, sipping as he pulled up a chair to sit down. 'You make good coffee.'

'Thanks.' she murmured. 'Now if you'll excuse me, I'll get dressed.'

A flicker of mild amusement stirred his eyes. He seemed in a flippant mood. 'No need to rush. And there's no need to be so embarrassed when a man admires a pretty woman like yourself.'

'Embarrassed?'

'Yes.' He glanced at her briefly then suggested softly, 'You are embarrassed about something, aren't you? Are you afraid of men—of me?'

'Of course not! And certainly not of you!'

She wondered why she felt so guilty at the hurt look that momentarily darkened his eyes but, pushing the guilt to the back of her mind, she held her head just a bit higher, 'Look, I've been thinking. Perhaps it's not such a good idea my coming to Twr Gwyn.'

He waved an arm impatiently, 'Don't start all that again! Why do you have to be such an obstinate little devil? You're becoming a thorn in my side.'

Hannah circled an arm in the air. 'I could make myself quite comfortable here. The barn's not too bad. I could make it fairly livable when the work on the house starts.'

'We've already been over all this. You'd be

far more comfortable at Twr Gwyn.'

Hannah managed a wry smile. 'It's aptly named, your house. White Tower . . . Funny, I always imagine it filled with Rapunzels.'

At that, he put back his head and laughed. 'It may have been when I was sixteen but I'm well past that stage now. Although . . .' he paused briefly, his voice softening and tempered with conviction—'seeing you in that sexy little shirt thing makes me feel very young again.' He grinned pausing slightly. 'The problem is I don't want to feel sixteen again.'

'No—seriously, I'd rather—' She broke off, the shrill ring of the telephone interrupting any further conversation.

Hurriedly she went to answer it, moving into the hall quickly with a muttered, 'Excuse me.' When Hannah picked up the receiver her heart froze again as the jagged breathing came once more down the line.

'Who is this? Will you stop phoning me? Who are you?'

'I still love you darling . . . .'

Suddenly Hannah was shaking. She recognized the voice now! She'd heard these soft words of love before but now they were gripping her heart like an avalanche of ice. Her lips felt so stiff she could hardly speak as she formed the name, *'Paul?'*

'Right first time. It's me—your loving husband.'

'You're not my husband now, Paul. What is

it you want? Why are you phoning me after all this time?'

There was a long pause and when at last he spoke again, his voice wavered a little. 'Because I think you're being totally unreasonable. You're not considering my position at all.'

'Position? What position? Paul, what are you talking about?'

She heard him laugh, shaky and wavering. 'Oh, you had me fooled for a while. I always knew there was someone else, but I could never catch you out. Now I know there's someone.'

'Paul! Stop it! Why are you doing this?'

Again, the awful sound of his laughter came down the line. 'It's what you're doing that's the trouble. But you're not going to get away with it, my darling. You are still my wife and no one else is going to have you.'

'Paul! I didn't—'

'By the way, darling, I was sorry to hear of your little accident the other day. The roads can be so dangerous these days.'

'The roads—'

Abruptly, he hung up.

Hannah replaced the receiver in a daze. It must be some terrible joke he was playing. But how did he know about the accident! Surely, it couldn't have been Paul who had been the driver of the other car? Would he try to harm her? She frowned. Why not? He was quite capable of it! She would never forget the brutal, bruising act of submission he called lovemaking. Oh, no! She shook her head. What was the matter with her? Why should he want to hurt her now? Surely, it must be some sick joke.

'What's happened? You look as white as a sheet.'

Hannah spun round to find Chris Talbot standing a couple of feet behind her. 'It's—it's nothing,' she stammered, 'it's just an old friend, that's all.'

He gave her a hard, level look as she stood there twisting a silver ring on her finger. 'I couldn't help overhearing the tail-end of it and it didn't sound very friendly to me.'

Hannah swallowed. Hearing Paul's voice again had shaken her badly and she desperately needed to regain her composure. She was afraid. She lifted her hand to push her hair from her eyes. She was probably over-reacting. Surely, there was no need for concern, and perhaps Fate was stepping in after all. If Paul was out to hurt her—take some form of demented revenge—then perhaps moving to Twr Gwyn was the safest bet. But, even as she told herself these things, if Paul was serious in his threats, she couldn't possibly involve Chris in yet another of her problems.

'Chris, I'm not coming with you. What's wrong with my booking in at the White Hart?'

She tried to sound determined, and if her voice lacked the volume, at least it was even.

Irritation deepened the lines of his mouth. 'For heaven's sake, stop arguing and get packed! Forget the White Hart or any other hotel. You know Twr Gwyn is the only sensible place to be. When are you going to face facts? You can't handle these changes on your own, and you can't stay here while the place is being pulled down around you. And I need your help when it comes to the layout and the arrangements. Now, come on, get changed, or do you want me to carry you out to the car dressed like that . . . ?' He laughed softly, the harshness fading from his face. 'We need each other. Stop worrying. I'll look after you.'

Hannah gave him a tight little smile. How often had she heard those words? In her experience people ought to look after themselves. Paul's family had protected him when he was making her life a misery. Her own father—loving as he'd been—had made her do things she didn't want to, simply because he was *looking after her*!

Chris waited, 'Well, are we going to stand here arguing all day?'

'I'd—I'd still like to give it a try on my own.'

'You can't!' His words held a finality as he stepped forward and grasped her by the arm. 'Now get ready and stop trying to fight me.'

There was a dead silence between them as they faced each other. 'You don't understand,' she murmured at last.

'I think I understand more than you realize. Now, be sensible and come with me to Twr Gwyn.'

'But—'

'*Do as you're told for once!* How will you survive at Tregarn without my help?'

Hannah bit her lip in grim silence, thinking bitterly that this kind of help was the last thing she needed. She held herself still, blue eyes glaring, yet painfully aware of the bald truth of his words.

After a moment or two she sighed. 'All right. I'll stay at Twr Gwyn until Tregarn is ready.'

His voice seemed to come from a long way away. 'You've been mixing with the wrong people for too long.'

He stepped forward and took her in his arms. Then suddenly, there was colour and light as his lips pressed against hers as she kissed him back. Hannah found herself putting all of her fears, her hopes, her dreams into that kiss. Chris lifted his head for a brief moment, his eyes disclosing delight and surprise, then his lips came down on hers again, beguiling her and utterly seducing her. No man should be allowed such power as this! It wasn't fair!

In the distance a car horn blared, bringing her back into focus. She swallowed hard. She was intelligent enough to know that men were predators, and this man—this man above all others—had more than his share of the predator's hunting instinct. He was ensnaring her with his soft words and his gentle, sensuous touch. And, ominously, he recognized this female's weakness to his bait.

Panic stepped in, sending her reeling from him, pushing him away, terrified to find that she was almost on the brink of betraying everything she had always held so fiercely.

'I must be crazy,' she cried, her voice rising as she struggled to resist her emotions. 'Women come too easily for you and I'm *never* going to be one of them!'

Chris held out his hand, his eyes like dark hollows. 'Why are you so scared? You *do* want me! I know you do! Tell me why you're so afraid.'

Hannah pushed him away, freeing herself from his touch, listening to her own voice as it cried out its protest. 'I'm not afraid of anyone! And—and don't ever try to—to kiss me like that again.'

'Ever is a long time.'

'I mean it! Don't ever lay a finger on me again. I know your type—one woman will never be enough for you!'

Desperately, she dredged up the control she needed to keep her head and managed a little shrug. 'Having me at Twr Gwyn would just suit your purpose, wouldn't it?'

'What purpose?'

'Having me at your beck and call. Is that

84

why your wife left you? Couldn't she keep up with your demands—or *your women?*'

Hannah held her breath, wishing she could bite out her tongue. What had possessed her to say such a cruel thing? She had thought that she could keep him at a distance with insults; that somehow she would be safe; but she hadn't meant to say such a dreadful thing as that.

Although his hands tightened around her, he kept a tight rein on his temper. 'Don't ever use Joyce's name in that context again,' he advised quietly. *'Do you hear me? Never!* One day you'll push me too far and I don't recommend it, lovely girl.' She felt his hold on her slacken. His face was ashen, drained, as he moved away. 'Now let's get you out of here before I change my mind.'

Too late she tried to draw her head back, but he'd reached out his hand and held her chin. 'Damn you, Hannah Jones!' His muttered curse was barely audible. 'You've a great deal to learn about me! You've been mixing with the wrong people for too long. You don't know me at all! Nor do you know what you want! But, one thing's for sure,' his voice lowered even more, 'there's something going on inside you that's turning you sour . . . hurting you . . . and, whatever the something is, I'll find it, and that's my solemn promise. Now, for the last time, get packed.'

He stepped back, his dismissal setting her

teeth on edge, more because he'd hit the nail on the head again than anything else. He turned away and walked out of the room and, after a moment, Hannah moved too, going upstairs to pack the rest of her things.

CHAPTER SEVEN

Twr Gwyn hadn't changed much. It was just as beautiful now as Hannah had remembered it. It was the kind of house which held a strange beauty, an undefined peacefulness. Her memories of it had been remote, lost, seeing it only from the distance of childhood, and now, seeing it again for the first time in years, she was not disappointed by its reality.

The August sun bathed everything around in its subtle shades of gold, and along the lawns, in high summer bloom, the rainbow clusters of shrubs grew in abundance.

'Here we are,' Chris muttered gruffly, stopping the Shogun in front of the house. 'Home sweet home.'

He got out, opening the rear door to lift out Hannah's large leather cases and then setting them down on the wide step. He'd hardly spoken a word to her since they set out from Tregarn and now, as he waited for her by the elaborately carved column, his long, regarding look took in her every move.

Hannah followed him slowly, walking up to the door with an apprehension that was mixed with a vague feeling of excitement. She wondered, too, even at this late stage, whether it was not too late for her to turn tail again and run.

She was still pondering undecidedly when the door opened to reveal the short, stocky figure of Twr Gwyn's housekeeper, Megan Davies.

'Oh, here you are. I was beginning to think you'd changed your mind after all.' The woman cast a shrewd eye over them, speaking in a voice that was low, yet pitched so that Hannah was left in no doubt who was the one to reckon with in the Talbot household.

'Show Hannah her room will you, Megan?' Chris glanced at his watch. 'Mickey can take her cases up while I check the stables.' He turned curtly to Hannah. 'I'll see you later when you've settled in. Megan will show you where everything is and if there's anything you need don't be afraid to ask.' Adding with heavy sarcasm, 'Your wish is our command.' He moved away, striding down the steps two at a time and turning just once to give her a look that was as cold as winter 'We'll have a chat later . . . over supper perhaps?'

'That would he nice, thank you,' Hannah returned without conviction.

'Perhaps we could clear up a few things.'

Puzzled, Hannah gave him a guarded look.

'A few things?'

'I'm an inquisitive man.'

She shrugged, not knowing what else to say and she glowered in frustrated silence as, grim-faced, he strode away.

Her room was at the end of a wide passage on the first floor and, as Hannah looked around, Megan fussed with the curtains, brushing away imaginary flecks of dust. The woman chattered on, explaining to Hannah the routine of the household. Things like meal-times, where things were kept and, most of all, how she liked things to be done, and woe betide anyone who rocked the smooth day-to-day running of her organization.

Hannah listened patiently, nodding now and then in agreement, and taking in everything about her new surroundings, not finding anything which she wouldn't have chosen for herself. Even a bowl of her favourite flowers had been set on the cabinet by the bed, the sweet perfume of the freesias filling the room.

Christian Langley Talbot had been thorough in his research—everything was exactly how she liked it.

The floor was covered in thick, raspberry-coloured carpet, complementing perfectly the pink and white of the walls. A large king-sized bed took up almost half the space, covered in a rosy pink duvet and piled with pillows.

When Megan had gone, Hannah sat herself down on the window-seat, resting her head against the wall and wondering what was in store for her now she was actually living here under his roof.

*   *   *

'Another coffee? Or would you like something stronger?'

'Mmm?' Hannah jerked her gaze from the fading light in the sky. 'No, coffee's fine, thanks.'

It was late in the evening. They'd dined earlier on a superb meal of tender steak, sweet new potatoes and crisp green salad. The night air was hot, humid, and now Megan Davies had cleared away the last of the dishes and they were together in the coolness of the terrace.

Hannah hadn't spoken much over dinner, she hadn't felt the need to. She had found herself enjoying the fascinating contemplation of Christian Talbot's good-looking face, and listening to his account of the stable's day.

Somehow, she felt caught up in circumstances over which she had no control, and she'd spent most of the evening trying to focus her attention on the things around her rather than on her inner self. Until they'd come out on the terrace, their conversation had been civil but pleasant and, as he handed her the coffee, it was as natural as if they had shared evenings like this all their lives.

He sat down. 'Here's to Tregarn,' he said, lifting his cup to his mouth.

Hannah glanced at him sharply. 'I'll drink to that,' she said, taking a sip. 'Here's hoping I'll soon be back where I belong—and out of your hair.'

'There's no need to humour me,' he stated, meeting her eyes.

She looked right back at him. 'I was just trying to make conversation.'

'I like your outfit, it suits you,' he said flatly.

Hannah smiled wryly. 'Now who's humouring who?'

Her glance swept over him. He was impeccably dressed. Tonight his slacks were light beige, with a dark-green shirt and striped silk club tie. He ignored her question and Hannah glanced away, but was then drawn back to him. He was still looking, his serious, thoughtful expression oddly mature and definitely unnerving. They remained that way, locked in silent communication across the table, until he spoke again some moments later. 'Now, let's get down to some serious talk.'

'I'm ready,' she said, wondering if retreat was more in order.

He took another sip of his coffee then said quietly, 'I'm interested in Paul Denton, tell me about him.'

Taken aback by his directness, Hannah replied shortly, 'Paul? There's nothing to tell.'

'There must be. Something must have gone wrong in the Garden of Eden and that surprises me,' he said, leaning back in his chair. 'The guy seemed perfect for you. Well off, promising career, all that sort of thing. I thought you would have been married forever. Why didn't you get along?'

Hannah hesitated, taking a breath and, after a long pause, she answered softly, 'We weren't suited.'

He shrugged slightly. 'That's an overworked cliché these days.' He glanced across. 'He was the kind of man you admired, wasn't he?'

'Yes.'

'Not like me, I was never your kind, was I? You made that plain often enough.'

'That's nonsense.'

'No it isn't. You made it crystal clear what you thought of us—us local boys, guys like Mike and me—especially Mike! God, what you did to him! We were nothing more than country yobs to relieve your boredom until you could go back to that jet-set mob you preferred as friends. You wouldn't waste your time on a bunch of clod-hoppers like us!'

Hannah met his hostile stare, her mouth tight and mutinous. 'I never thought of you like that—or Mike!'

'I didn't notice you beating a path to my door.'

She let out a small, derisive laugh. 'No one could get near to your door! You had enough

91

to cope with with all your Talbot groupies! Tell the truth for once, you never even noticed me, did you?'

He laughed mockingly. 'Oh, I noticed you— I didn't miss a thing.' She felt the impact of his glance as he looked at her. 'So what went wrong?' he asked scathingly. 'Surely, Paul Denton had all the credentials necessary to make him the perfect husband for you?'

Hannah put her cup down on the small table between them. Her blue eyes glinted dangerously as she bit back the words that were springing impulsively to her lips, of the fact that the serpent in the Garden of Eden was Chris Talbot himself. 'Do we have to go into all this now?'

'Yes, we do,' he answered quietly. 'I want to know. I want to know what kind of man he is.' Hannah looked across at him, and caught him watching her with a sombre expression. 'I've always wondered what makes Hannah Jones tick. We've known each other since we were kids, spatting like cat and dog whenever our paths crossed, and yet . . . I always hoped there was something more behind that plastic image of yours.'

It was a moment before Hannah found her voice. 'Is it that important?'

'Yes, it is.' He drank again and drained his cup. 'I want to know what's so special about the guy, special enough to keep a girl like you interested.'

'What's the point in all this? You're not going to believe anything I say.'

'Try me.'

'I'd—I'd like to, but sometimes . . . you're so . . . so wrong about me . . . so unfeeling . . .'

His dark eyes flashed, and she saw the fires he kept so closely banked blaze brightly for a second then die away. He nodded bitterly. 'I wondered what has made me that way.'

Hannah turned away from his pitiless dark eyes. Her hands were unsteady as she picked up her coffee, taking a sip and putting it down again. She looked back at him to see the subdued lighting glinting on his blond hair, casting shadows across his cheekbones, making them seem more prominent. If it was possible, he looked more attractive than ever and Hannah felt her stomach muscles tighten.

'If you have so little regard for me, why are you doing all this to help me?' she asked, bewildered. 'I could have stayed at the White Hart. My being here doesn't affect your twenty-four acres.'

'I know. But I suppose it's to convince myself that I'd been mistaken in you all this time,' he answered, fingering a splinter of cane on the arm of the chair.

'And that's all it is? To prove to yourself that I'm still the same? That you haven't been wrong in your judgement of me?' He smiled slightly, enigmatically, not answering and Hannah put her hand over her eyes, feigning tiredness. 'Look, do we have to go on with this conversation?'

'I'm afraid so. I've already told you I'm inquisitive and I just need to clear a few things in my mind. You see, I've been wondering about this husband of yours for a long time, and what it takes to crack the ice with you.' He picked up her cup and held it out to her. 'Here, finish your drink. I hate to see good coffee going to waste.'

Hannah turned her face away so he put the cup down again.

'How long were you married?' he asked, resuming the inquisition again.

'Almost two years,' Hannah replied, clearing her throat.

'What was he like? Intelligent? Amusing? Boring? A good lover?'

'Stop!' Hannah exclaimed. 'For heaven's sake, stop! I'm tired, and this conversation's getting us nowhere.'

'Maybe not for you, but I find it extremely interesting.' His tone was tinged with irony, but perhaps Hannah was imagining it. 'And you still haven't answered the most intriguing question of all yet.'

'Which is?'

'What went wrong?'

She stood up quickly, her blue eyes glittering like iced diamonds. How dared he assume that she would expose her inner self like this? 'I've had enough of this!'

But Chris was on his feet too, his jaw rigid and his expression unyielding. 'Running away again?'

'I'm not running from anything!'

'Then answer my question—it's quite a reasonable one.'

Hannah inhaled deeply. Her mouth had a sour taste and her heart felt as heavy as lead. She paused to consider for a moment, then a little desperately, she murmured, 'Very well, if I tell you will it be the end of all this?'

'That depends on your answer.'

'I'll risk it.' She inhaled again, summoning control, then said quickly, 'The circumstances are . . . perhaps a little unusual.'

Chris waited a moment, studying her, then he prompted, 'Well, go on, don't stop there. How unusual?'

Hannah swallowed hard. 'It didn't work with Paul because, you see, I love someone else; I suppose I always will.'

Lord, that was true enough!

His mouth tightened and his gaze flicked over her, steely, dispassionately. 'If that's the case—if you loved someone else—why did you wind up with him in the first place?' he asked grimly. 'And who is this other man?' Where is he now? And did Denton know about him?'

'No! Nobody knows! And I must have been stark raving crazy to tell you—I don't know why I did!'

'Then why did you?' he demanded. 'And

where is this man now?'

'I—it was all a long time ago!'

'Tell me about it.'

'No! That's all I'm prepared to say! I've answered your question now leave it alone! I'm going to bed! Goodnight.'

'Not until you've told me where lover boy is now!'

'I—I can't.'

Oh, how she longed to tell him exactly where *lover boy* was! *That he was less than two feet away from her right now!*

Panic was driving her and Hannah fled past him into the dining-room, part of her wanting to run a million miles away from his probing questions, and another part longing to tell him the whole truth of her painful feelings.

She flew across the hall and up the stairs until she reached the privacy of her room, leaning against the door and closing her eyes, grateful for the silence.

She wondered what to do. For one thing it was easy to say that staying here at Twr Gwyn would all be over soon, and yet another to have to face Chris's stinging questions. Why, oh why, did she have to blurt out that dreadful confession? What was happening to her? Why did he always make her act so irrationally—so *illogically*?

After a few minutes she straightened up and, sitting down at her dressing-table, she smoothed her hair with shaking hands and cleansed her face, her heart leaping a few moments later as she heard the soft tap on her door.

She squared her shoulders, looking round. 'Who is it?' As if she didn't know!

'Are you all right?' Chris's voice came from the other side, softly.

'Of course, I'm all right.'

'May I come in?'

'No.'

'Oh, come on, Hannah, open the door. I hate talking through a piece of wood. You always ran away when you were a kid if something upset you, remember? And it was invariably me then.'

Hannah toyed with her comb, his reference to their childhood almost finishing off her fraught nerves, but even so, she crossed the room and opened the door. 'Have you come to start round two?'

'Wrong,' he muttered, his hand reaching through the narrow space and winding around her hair. 'I've come to apologize. I didn't mean to upset you, but I've waited a long time to ask those questions and I wanted a few straight answers.'

She gave a shaky laugh. 'And are you satisfied now?'

'No, I'm even more curious. Who's this other man, the one you say you love?'

Hannah sighed, her defence mechanism almost exhausted as she murmured wearily,

97

'Chris, no more tonight, please. I'm tired and I want to go to sleep.'

He cupped her chin but she averted her eyes, shaking her head as he sighed in mock sympathy. 'I was hoping to melt some of that ice by forcing you to talk about it—bring it into the open. But all I've done is to upset you. Can't you tell me who he is? Is he married?'

'No—no more—please.' Hannah eyed him wearily, suddenly dreadfully worn-out. 'And you haven't really upset me, I'm just tired.'

'I will prove something to you one of these fine days. I'll show you what loving a real man can do.' He kissed her lightly on the forehead. 'Goodnight . . . lovely girl.'

Hannah closed the door and turned back towards her bed. As she climbed in Hannah tried to remind herself that his interest in her was nothing more than a taste for forbidden fruit—a gauntlet thrown down to see how far he could go with her. That's all it could be because, no matter how attractive he found her, how much of a puzzle, he had never loved her.

That crown had been placed on someone else's head—Joyce's—the girl he had once married! Hannah Jones was second-best! Joyce had been his first choice! Joyce had been the woman he loved! And, no matter how deep her feelings lay, the thought of that was like a knife through her heart.

*   *   *

The days passed by quickly enough and, in spite of everything, Hannah found herself beginning to relax. And although she hardly dared to admit it, even to herself, it was making all the difference now that Chris had placed himself in charge.

During the fine summer days, when she wasn't at Tregarn, she tried to immerse herself in useful occupation, helping out around the house, or giving a hand in the stables, and loving the tight-knit way the stable lads, trainers and horses all worked together.

Slowly, but surely, it seemed Chris was taking over more and more of her life. In one way she was glad of it, but in another, was irritated by it. They were neither lovers nor friends and, wherever she went around the estate, he seemed to be there, watching her, amused by her situation.

They settled into a sort of routine. While Chris spent a great deal of his time with the horses, when her car had been repaired, Hannah would drive over to Tregarn at least once a day, not only to keep her eye on things, but to take over any equipment that the workmen needed, things like rolls of wire or tins of paint. In fact, anything that would fit into the boot and back seat of her car. At least, this way, she could see for herself how Tregarn was coming along.

*   *   *

Hannah went out into the forecourt after breakfast to do her usual run and was just about to open the garage door when she spotted Mickey Roberts fidgeting around the gates.

Mickey was the man Chris had designated as foreman for Tregarn, and as he strode quickly across the flagged courtyard towards her, Hannah couldn't fail to notice the agitated look on his face, dimming his usually cheery smile.

'Can't use your car today, miss,' he said, clearing his throat and wiping his forehead on his shirt sleeve. 'Mr Talbot's given orders that we take it in for a service.'

Hannah frowned slightly. Although Chris never said Hannah knew how much he hated her going off to Tregarn every day on her own. She wondered now, looking at Mickey's worried face, whether sending her car for a service was just another ploy to keep her under his thumb at Twr Gwyn.

'What about the new set of paint brushes, aren't they waiting for them?'

'It's OK, miss, Jed's already taken 'em. He went over in the truck about an hour ago, thought he'd save you the trouble.'

She stood for a moment chewing on her lip, then, hearing a distant neighing sound,

100

inspiration struck. 'That's all right, Mickey, I'll go over to Tregarn anyway. I'll take one of the horses.' And, before he could answer, she raced past him and towards the stable.

Scratching his head, the foreman watched her go. He knew he was in for it now. Mr Talbot had given strict orders that she mustn't go to Tregarn today. But what could he do? He couldn't very well drag her back, could he?

He shrugged and went off towards the stables muttering. He wanted no part of this. Out of the corner of his eye, he could see one of the young stable lads helping her to saddle up a grey mare and he frowned again as she galloped off across the field. The fat was in the fire now! Mr Talbot wouldn't like this one bit!

Tregarn was almost unrecognizable. Dust, smells and curses filled the air as the bulldozer demolished what remained of the old barn, and already half the rear of the house had been ripped out, her furniture in store at Twr Gwyn. Hannah wandered round in a kind of dazed blankness. So much had changed. This morning even the outbuildings had gone. They were nothing more than a pile of bricks and mortar now, and she stood silently by as two men heaped shovelful after shovelful of rubble into a rusty metal skip.

Looking about her at what remained of her home and seeing everything now in this gutted state, she found it almost impossible to imagine how the new Tregarn could ever rise again. But rise it would, she was convinced of that. And when it did, perhaps she would see it as a new sign of life, both in her father's dreams and in her own.

Reining the mare, Hannah leaned against the fence thinking hard. She had heard no more from Paul. Perhaps at last, he'd accepted that he was no longer a part of her life. And, moments later, her thoughts turned as always to Chris.

Since that time he'd kissed her, he had treated her exactly as he always had. There was not a flicker of an eye or a secret glance to indicate that he thought any more of Hannah than he did of his horses. Come to think of it, he probably thought more of them—he gave them more attention.

All her sharp perceptions told her that the staff around Twr Gwyn must suspect *something* in their strange relationship. They knew their boss too well to believe that it could be merely a platonic arrangement.

A fly flew on to her hand, bringing her back to the present with a bump. Head bent, her thoughts swirling around in her head like phantoms, she brushed it away, and as she did so, a blurred movement in the distance caught her eye.

She looked up, squinting her eyes in the sunlight at the horse and rider and recognizing at once the broad-shouldered, shirt-sleeved figure of Chris Talbot looming ever larger across the fields towards her. Hannah swore eloquently under her breath. Damn! Couldn't she be alone even here—not even for one minute? Did he always have to show up when she was at her most vulnerable?

Chris eyed her with muted anger as he approached, and his disbelieving black gaze swept over her, lighting unerringly on the slim-hipped shape of her denims and the black hair tumbling below her scarf.

He reined in, his jaw set stubbornly. 'Well,' he said wryly. 'Having fun?'

'Wonderful fun.' Her look dared him to make something of it.

'Didn't you get my message?'

Hannah shrugged slightly. 'What message?'

'I told Mickey that I wanted you to stay at Twr Gwyn today, I hadn't expected you to go tearing off like this.'

'Why not? You know I always come to Tregarn. Why shouldn't I come today?'

'I've had a call from Galbraith, he'll have everything ready to sign tomorrow afternoon and we can start on the annexe proper.'

'Good.'

He watched her from the height of his horse, leaning forward on the saddle and his gaze drifting over her. 'We need to talk. Have you finished here? Will you come back to Twr Gwyn with me?'

Hannah shrugged but didn't reply as she remounted the grey. Twisting in the saddle to look at him she asked, 'What time do we have to be at Galbraith's tomorrow?'

The roan shifted restively beneath him and, as Chris controlled the animal with his legs, the leather saddle creaked dully. 'Two o'clock, but I won't be able to come with you.'

'Why not?'

'Something's come up. I have to fly over to Ireland this afternoon, that's why I wanted you at Twr Gwyn today. We need a final discussion on the split between the twin and double rooms before we hand the plans over to the builder.'

'I reckon eight twin and four double,' Hannah responded, adding mockingly, 'that is, if my partner agrees.'

He gave a small indifferent shrug. 'Sounds about right, but it's up to you.'

They set off at walking pace. Hannah didn't know whether to feel relieved or irritated by his news. Deep down she was conscious of a small pang of regret to hear that he was going away. And Hannah knew exactly why she felt the way she did. 'How long will you be in Ireland?'

'It may take me a couple of days. As it is, you'll have to drive into Cardiff by yourself, sign your part of the papers, and I'll call in to sign my half when I get back.'

'Can't it wait until you get back anyway?' A small voice was already nagging in the back of her head. What could possibly interest him in

Ireland? Unless? Suddenly, a wave of unreasoning jealousy swept over her. Joyce was in Ireland! Was it Joyce he was going to see? Was he still in touch with her? Did he still love her after all this time? She drew a deep breath and asked impatiently, 'Surely, Galbraith can wait for a couple of days.' Hannah surprised herself. In spite of her sudden inner turmoil, her tone was quite even.

'No. I don't want to hold things up for him more than I can help, he's pulled out all the stops for us as it is.'

They rode on in silence. Hannah hadn't realized just how tense she had been about the thought of him going off like this. She was suddenly afraid. The feeling worried her but, she thought ruefully, there was not a lot she could do about it.

She was tempted to ask him to take her with him but, of course, she didn't. Instead, she turned, looking at his profile, surveying the perfect bone structure that gave his face such an angular strength. 'Will my car be ready soon?' she asked lamely.

'I've decided to take that wreck off the road for good: it's had its day and it's good for nothing now except the scrap yard. You can use the Mercedes.'

She was cornered again and she knew it. He was right about her car, it had had its day. It had been on its last legs to start with and the accident had sealed its fate. But she had no other way of getting into Cardiff from Twr Gwyn, unless she made the marathon journey by bus.

He was waiting for her answer. 'All right.' Her surrender was almost inaudible.

A small wry smile tugged at the corners of his mouth. 'I hope you don't fret too much while I'm gone.'

Hannah gave a light shrug. 'I'll try to struggle through.'

'Don't struggle too much,' he said mildly. 'I'd hate you to admit you'll miss me.'

'I won't.'

'Not even a little?'

'Not even a little.'

'You're not doing very much for my ego.'

'Your ego doesn't need any boosting from me.'

'How can you say that when you know how sensitive I am?'

'It could work both ways—will you miss me?'

'I'll have a lot to do in Ireland, but I'll try.'

'Don't strain yourself.'

'I won't.'

They rode on. Would she miss him? The thought of not seeing him, even for so short a time, was already making her feel cold and empty inside. Miss him? Already that lonely knife was slashing away at her insides.

'Be careful, Chris, I'd—I'd—' She said the words before she could stop herself, breaking

106

off abruptly at his astonished glance and mumbling brokenly, 'Well, just be careful.'

He threw back his head, laughing loudly. 'Good heavens, that almost sounds genuine,' he said, then still laughing, 'Come on, I have a plane to catch.'

He slapped the mare and flicked the roan into long galloping strides that quickly took both riders and horses back over the valley to Twr Gwyn.

CHAPTER EIGHT

As she dined alone, Hannah was already finding the house too quiet without him. He'd driven off to Rhoose airport hours ago, leaving her with a brief kiss on the forehead and now, remembering his kiss, slight as it was, a feeling of such loneliness swept through her that she got up restlessly. Bad feelings had plagued her all through her solitary dinner, her stomach lurching constantly with jealousy. Had he really gone to Ireland on business? Or was he with his ex-wife even as Hannah sat here alone . . . thinking of him . . . missing him so dreadfully?

She strolled out on to the terrace, her sombre glance falling upon the U-shaped lawn that wrapped around a miniature ornamental lake, and admiring its limpid beauty. She knew

Chris was far from poor but she still felt surprise at the luxury of everything.

She wandered back into the dining-room, wondering how long she would be able to stand the boredom and emptiness his absence had brought. Perhaps, tomorrow, she would tie back the clematis. She'd noticed how everyone brushed against it as they went through the patio door and, if it wasn't tied back, it could be damaged. Then there was the lily-pond, the reeds were taking over—

Hannah pulled herself up. What on earth was she thinking about? She was already looking on Twr Gwyn as her home! It was ridiculous! There was nothing of herself here, apart from two suitcases of clothes. This was Chris Talbot's white tower!

At last, restlessness drove her to bed.

*　　　*　　　*

After breakfast next morning, Mickey Roberts brought the Mercedes to the front of the house and, on the long drive into Cardiff, Hannah found herself going over in her mind exactly what she would say to Paul if he should bother her again.

She quickly signed the papers in Galbraith's office and immediately drove straight back to Twr Gwyn.

The rest of the day passed uneventfully enough but she wished Chris would ring to let her know what time he'd be coming home. He didn't ring, nor did he the next night either. The two days stretched into three, four, and then five. She waited and waited, running to the phone at the first sound, then turning away, disappointed, to find that the call was not for her.

But if Chris didn't ring, then neither did Paul. For a while she'd been afraid that he would start to pester her all over again, but the reassuring silence continued. Maybe something—or someone—else had taken his attention. Whatever the reason, Hannah was profoundly grateful.

On the fifth night she went upstairs earlier than usual. It was sultry, the air thick with humidity, and although she bathed in cool water, she was sticky again within five minutes. It was too early and too hot to sleep so she slipped into her lightest, coolest robe and sat by the open window in search of a breeze. She curled up in a cane chair, throwing off the over-padded cushions and wrapping a fine cotton shawl along its back. A breath of wind fanned her cheeks, making her sigh in relief as she listened to the sounds of the night.

Somewhere, an owl hooted and, faintly on the still air, came the sound of a cricket. It was like a lullaby. Her eyelids drooped, not quite dozing, but sinking into a peaceful lethargy where time passed unregarded.

She must have been day-dreaming like that

for over an hour when the sound of a car's wheels crunched on the gravel below. She opened her eyes to the flash of headlights, making her flinch and turn away from the blinding light.

She sat up, her heart leaping as the tall, blond-haired, broad-shouldered man climbed out of the Shogun and slammed the door. The moonlight wasn't bright, but she didn't need light to know who the man was.

She heard the downstairs door open and close, and waited to hear the sound of his footsteps coming up the stairs. When he knocked softly on her door, her answering 'Come in, Chris', was a low whisper of sound as she turned her face towards him.

'Everything all right?'

'Yes.'

'Any problems while I've been away?' The questions were deceptively conversational. Chris was looking down at her, his strong face relaxed into a smile.

Hannah was completely awake now, getting up out of the chair and taking a small step forward. 'No, no problems as far as I know. How—how was Ireland?'

'Cooler than here.'

'And how—how did your business—er—turn out?'

'Such as?'

'I meant, was your . . . business . . . satisfactory?'

His smile deepened blandly. 'Quite satisfactory, thanks.' Then adding with a trace of ironic amusement, 'Is there something wrong?'

Hannah moved restlessly. 'No, why should anything be wrong?' She cleared her throat. He clearly wasn't prepared to give much away about his mysterious trip so she tried another tack. 'Megan's gone to bed, would you like me to get you something to eat?'

'Thanks, but no. I had something on the plane and I had a huge meal before I left.'

'I see . . .' She smiled woodenly. 'Did you stay—do you have friends—family—in Ireland?'

'Both. Friends and family.' Dark eyes sparkled above the fine cheekbones.

'Good friends?'

'I like to think so.'

'Does—' Hannah cleared her throat again, dreading to ask the next question. 'Does Joyce still live in Ireland?'

'Yes.'

She swallowed, stung by his admission. So it *hadn't* been a business trip alone! 'Was she—is she well?'

'Perfectly, thank you,' Chris returned crisply. 'But why this sudden concern with my affairs? You haven't shown much interest before.'

'I'm just being conversational,' she defended. 'I wondered what it could be that

111

kept you in Ireland for five days when you told me you would be back in two.'

The expression in his eyes deepened. 'I didn't think you'd be the type to count the days.'

'Well, I—I—' Hannah floundered into silence, not wanting to betray for even an instant that, if he'd asked her, she could tell him the number of seconds, too.

'Something came up, it couldn't be helped.'

'I see.' She set her lips, then asked, 'Why didn't you telephone? I waited to hear from you.'

'I didn't have the time.'

Somehow Hannah thought that was only part of the reason. 'That's not much of an excuse.'

'It's the only one I've got,' he replied with a grin. 'Anyway, what are you doing cooped up here? The house looked so dark when I came up the drive that I thought you must have gone out somewhere, then I saw your light and thought perhaps you were already asleep.'

'It's too hot to sleep.'

He grunted in agreement, reaching for her cheek with his hand and stroking it gently. 'I believe you've missed me a little.'

'I have . . . a little.'

He paused, looking down at her. 'Good.' His voice was low, the teasing gone. 'Because I've missed you, too. And I owe you an apology.'

'Oh?'

'Yes. While I was in Ireland I ran into Mike. I'm sorry, Hannah, for the terrible things I accused you of. He told me the truth about your relationship and I feel so ashamed.'

Hannah shook her head dismissively, glad he knew the truth about one thing at least. 'It's all right—we all make mistakes.'

'Yes, we do, and I'd like to make it up to you.' He drew her towards him and smiled a little as she tensed. 'There's nothing to be afraid of, Hannah.'

Hannah gave a shaky laugh. 'I'm not afraid, Chris.'

'I thought you might have been out on the town on a lovely evening like this.'

'No. I thought about it, but I changed my mind.'

'Are you afraid to go out?'

'Of course not!'

She turned her face away in case he read the lie in her eyes. He sensed her fear but how could she explain it? How could she tell him that she felt safe here? That she didn't want to move away from Twr Gwyn, and that she was afraid of someone who had hurt her a long time ago, and that he might come back and frighten her again?

'I think you are. There's something, I know there is. You're afraid, and I can feel it, yet whenever I try to bring it up, you tense up again like you are now. There's a distance

113

between us and I don't like it. I don't like it when you hide things from me. Can't you understand, I want to help?'

'You've helped me enough as it is.'

'Why do you keep me at arm's length when I know, deep down, you feel *something* for me?' He tilted her chin, forcing her to look at him. 'You do feel something, don't you?'

'It isn't . . . something I find easy to talk about. I've always equated such feelings with love, and I—and I—' She sighed deeply, trailing off. What else could she possibly say without giving her true feelings away?

He became suddenly still, his face cold and remote. 'Ah, yes, love . . . the old enemy. Which reminds me, what about this other man—the one you're in love with . . . are you going to tell me about him?'

His question came at her like a whip, its rawness flicking at her most painful and sensitive part—her heart. She almost winced physically at the pain of it as she whispered, 'He—he doesn't love me, he—doesn't know how I feel . . .' Hannah licked her nervous, dry lips, unable to look him in the face.

Chris paused, watching her as her words sank in. He was seeing her for the first time with all her defences down and a shudder ran through her. Her pride in shreds. She could hardly bear it as tension gripped her in an iron fist.

'Then . . . that makes two of us,' he murmured bitterly at last.

'What?' She stared at him uncomprehendingly.

'We're both in the same boat. Your love is unrequited and so is mine. We're two lost sheep you and I, Hannah, neither of us having the love we want . . . so, we might just as well comfort each other.'

A smile curved his mouth, inviting her to share his ironic amusement and Hannah stared blankly at him. 'So you—you *are* in love with someone?' she asked hoarsely.

'Very much, but she loves someone else.'

And in his eyes Hannah saw the pain he was unable to hide.

A tide of misery flooded through her. She had been able to hold out against all the torments he had inflicted, but now, this was far too much to bear.

There was silence until Chris touched her again, bending his head and brushing her lips with his. 'There's no point in either of us being lonely, is there . . . ?'

'Chris.' She lifted her eyes to face him squarely. 'Please don't ask me to do something we both might regret.'

'You won't regret it, I promise.'

'Don't make a promise you might not be able to keep. What happens when Tregarn is finished, when it's time for me to move back?'

'There's no need for you to move back.' Slight irritation deepened his mouth. 'How often do I have to remind you? I intend to run

115

the place with you—you can't do it on your own.'

'Perhaps not,' Hannah responded stubbornly. 'But I mean to try.' Desperation edged her tone. 'Don't you understand? I've never supported myself in my life, but I'm trying to now. You're taking me over, Chris, just like Dad—and Paul. If I give in to you now, I'll be finished.' She broke off, wondering how to put into words the things she wanted to say. She circled her arm undecidedly. 'You'll soon be off to your next . . .'

Chris glared at her. 'My next what? What do you take me for? Do you think I'm the kind of man who'll say, "Well, thank you, Ms Jones, it was great fun but now I'm off to look for someone else"? Can't you see that I'm serious about you—about Tregarn?'

Hannah gave him a tight little smile. 'You're very plausible. And I seem to have heard that somewhere before.'

His face was dark with impatience now. 'What do you want, Hannah? Is there anything I can say that will convince you that I'm no longer the kind of man you once thought you knew—the kind of man who collects girls like scalps?'

Tiredly, Hannah pressed her fingers against her eyes. He wasn't used to argument. 'I didn't mean it that way.'

'Then what way *did* you mean it?'

She gave a small sigh. What was the use?

116

How could she ever tell him how much she wanted—needed—his love? But that love belonged to someone else. 'I don't know.'

The harsh look faded from his face and he held her again in his arms. 'Look,' he said softly, 'I respect your need to try to run Tregarn. But it isn't logical or realistic, is it? All I'm asking you to do is lean on me for a little while, that's not too much to ask, is it?' Hannah shook her head but made no answer and Chris caught a strand of her dark hair and wound it through his fingers. 'Stop trying to be so independent and think of me for a change.'

'I am thinking about you.'

'Then think how tired I'd get worrying about you all alone over there.'

He held her close again, his hands stroking along her back. From outside came the rumble of thunder, a storm was on its way. It seemed to reverberate in tune to her inner tumult; to the pounding of her heart; to the innate desire that this man created inside her. She had no place to run now, but she no longer had the wish to run away. She was where she wanted to be—where she belonged—in Chris's arms.

CHAPTER NINE

Over the next few weeks they reached a sort of compromise. Tregarn was almost ready and to

Hannah, loving Chris for so long, it seemed that these last dwindling days seemed to be the only continuous thread of her life, giving her something to hold on to. During this time, Hannah felt a deep happiness begin to form within her.

She was given more and more to do around Twr Gwyn and she even persuaded Chris to let her loose on his paperwork, working on his books for three or four days a week.

At first, he had been reluctant. 'What on earth do you know about book-keeping?' had been his gruff reaction to her offer.

'I took a course on it at college.'

'But books are a serious job,' he'd muttered irritably. 'My accounts aren't something I'd let an amateur play around with.'

'My dad let me do his,' she snapped in return.

He'd smiled wryly. 'Is that supposed to give me confidence?'

In the end, however, he'd relented and it worked well for both of them. It gave Chris more time to see to the estates—both his own and Tregarn. It released him from the tedium of book-keeping and gave him the freedom to do what he liked best—to work with his horses.

And it worked for Hannah, too. At least she felt she was useful. And she felt different somehow. She no longer felt like the empty-headed social butterfly she had once been.

118

And, had she but known it, even the stable lads were amazed at the change in the Hannah Jones they once knew, commenting on the fact whenever Hannah did something else that would surprise them. She found Chris watching her sometimes, too. His face would hold an unbelieving look, as if he no longer recognized this new Hannah Jones either.

For the last couple of weeks, Twr Gwyn had been in the throes of concentrated training. Chris's decision to enter three of his more promising sprinters into the Novices' chase at Haydock Park meant that he spent more and more time out in the pastures and less and less time around the house. Now they were ready and two hours earlier she had waved goodbye as Chris and the boys had loaded the horse-boxes to make the long drive up to Liverpool. Twr Gwyn, after the clamour and excitement of the last week, was strangely quiet.

Hannah made her way into Chris's office, determined to spend the rest of the day working on Tregarn's new lay-out for the dining-room. She was alone. Megan wasn't in today either, getting over a heavy cold that had persisted for over a week and, apart from making sure Chris had everything he needed for the race meeting, Hannah had worn herself to a frazzle answering the phone. It never seemed to stop ringing and she was already feeling irritated as she looked up from the lay-out as it rang again for the umpteenth time.

119

'Hello! Twr Gwyn!'

She waited for the usual request to speak to Chris but, this time, no one answered. The only sound was a slow, deep breathing on the other end of the line.

Her heart sank. 'Hello! Hello!' Her voice sharpened. 'For goodness sake, Paul, don't start your silly tricks again!'

She heard the quiet click as the caller hung up and Hannah pursed her lips as she placed the phone back on its cradle. She sat back, surveying the instrument thoughtfully. Common sense told her it could have been a wrong number, but she knew deep down it wasn't, and a sudden chill swept over her.

She turned away to concentrate on her work, but still the feeling of menace hung over her. For the first time in weeks she felt threatened again. Her concentration evaporated. Suddenly she felt stifled and needed to get out into the air. Even more, she wanted Chris. She wanted him here, beside her. She wanted to feel his reassuring presence consoling her. But it was no use wishing for Chris. He was halfway up the M6 on his way to Liverpool, and she was alone.

Getting up from her work, she wandered into the kitchen to make herself some coffee, sitting quietly and trying to gather herself together. Her fingers drummed nervously against the mug and her clear blue eyes held a perturbed expression. Why was she suddenly

120

feeling as though an axe was about to fall? She was being ridiculous! The call was probably nothing more than what she'd thought in the beginning—a wrong number. She hoped so! Lord, she hoped so! She hoped against hope that her instincts were wrong and that it hadn't been Paul Denton at the end of the line.

Hannah gave herself a mental shake. She had work to do and she mustn't waste her time on such negative thoughts. Draining her cup and thrusting her sombre fears aside, she went back into the office and turned her attention to the lay-out.

The next day, Hannah quelled the familiar shiver as she heard the phone ringing from downstairs and Megan calling her from the hallway.

'Hannah! Telephone!'

'I'm coming, Megan!'

Hannah ran her fingers through her disordered hair as she made her way downstairs and, trembling a little, she picked up the phone. 'Hello!'

'Hannah?' The voice sounded far away but she recognized it at once.

'Yes, Paul,' she answered, swallowing convulsively.

'There's something we have to talk about.'

'I—I—don't think so, Paul.'

'Oh yes, we do my precious. That little exercise in the road was just a warning! And you'd better tell your boy-friend to keep away

121

from you or I'll get him, too—'

'No! Paul! Why are you doing this? Why can't you leave us alone?'

'If I can't have you, no one can!'

'Paul—you're mad! Crazy!'

'No, Hannah, you're the one who's mad. You should never have hurt me the way you did, knowing how much I care for you. Come back to me. Come back where you belong. Forget Tregarn—forget Chris Talbot—and all those dreams of your father's.'

'I can't! I'm—I'm sorry, Paul.'

'You will be sorry if you don't come back to me—and Talbot even more so!' Helplessly, Hannah listened to the shrill sound of rage building up in her ex-husband's voice. 'If you come back to me, I won't harm him. But, if you don't—'

Hannah gathered her strength, his threats inspiring her fragile confidence, sending her words rushing out like a torrent. 'You mustn't hurt him, Paul! He's done you no harm! Look, if you like, I'll—I'll meet you somewhere and we'll talk this over. Shall we do that? Shall we talk, Paul?'

She waited as Paul made a strange little sound that passed as a laugh. 'Yes, precious one, we'll talk. I'll meet you at Tregarn this afternoon.'

There was a click and the line went dead.

To steady herself she gripped the edge of the table and leaned against it. Oh, dear Lord, she was frightened! How could he put her through all this again? Why couldn't he leave her alone? She'd had more than four years of this nightmare and now Chris was in danger, too!

Well, she thought grimly, gathering herself together, she would put an end to it soon, because if she didn't, she *would* go mad!

'I've made some coffee, you look as though you need it.'

Hannah jerked her head to Megan and gave a feeble smile. 'Thanks, Megan, I think I do.'

She followed the housekeeper into the kitchen, picking up the odour of chest liniment and cough drops from the woman in front. And, as Megan handed her a cup, the black bird-like eyes pierced Hannah in silent speculation.

'Who was that on the phone?' Megan asked sharply. 'What did he say to make you look so pale?'

Wearily, Hannah shook her head. 'It's someone playing a very sick joke. I feel I ought to talk to someone about him—the police, perhaps.'

'Is it that bad?'

'I'm afraid it is.'

'Then why don't you talk to Chris about it— he'll know what to do?'

'Perhaps I will, when he gets back.'

'He's already back.'

Hannah looked up quickly. 'I didn't know!

123

Where is he?'

Megan studied Hannah closely with those piercing eyes of hers. 'They left Haydock earlier than they expected and got home during the small hours. He didn't go to bed. He's down at the stables now. There's a new colt coming later today. Why don't you go into the sitting-room with your coffee and I'll give him a ring?'

'I will, Megan, and—thanks.'

In the sitting-room waiting for Chris, Hannah stood by the window looking out. From the very beginning she should have told Chris about Paul. She should have cut it out like a rotten branch when he'd first started to phone her. It was a nightmare! But then, her reflective thoughts took another, more ominous, direction; if she *did* tell Chris she would only implicate him in more of her troubles.

And Paul had threatened to harm him!

No! This was something she had to sort out for herself! She had to prevent Paul from hurting Chris—even if it meant going back to a husband she despised!

She took long breaths of steadying air, looking towards the stables and at the single file of racehorses as they were led into the pasture for their morning exercise. A few minutes later, as she stood lost in her thoughts, she heard the door click and Chris came into the room.

'Megan tells me you're upset. Something about a phone call—are you all right?'

She looked up at him, managing a tiny smile. 'Yes.'

'What's it all about?'

She shrugged slightly. 'It's—it's really nothing. Just a nuisance call.'

She glanced up to see how deeply his dark eyes were studying her, taking in her troubled expression and her pale cheeks and, after a moment, he asked crisply, 'Well, will you tell me about it?'

'There's really nothing to tell.'

'Are you sure it's a nuisance call? Megan sounded worried. She said she recognized the man—said he'd rung up before.'

'He has—once or twice . . .'

'Do you know who it is?'

'Oh, yes, I know who it is.'

There was a long pause. He seemed to be probing her thoughts—suspicious. And his dark eyes were studying her clinically. 'Is it your mysterious Mr Wonderful?'

Hannah grew cold again. He was getting it all wrong. She wasn't handling this at all well. 'No! It's my ex-husband. Let me explain—'

She got no further as Chris's voice broke in harshly. 'If he keeps phoning you he must still be interested. And you can't play with a man's emotions like this and expect him not to react in some way.'

'You've got it all wrong, Chris.'

125

'Have I? Then explain.'

'I will if you'll give me the chance—'

She broke off as the telephone rang again from the hall. Chris fumed slowly and Hannah met his eyes, her face calm and mask-like but her insides churning so much that she almost felt giddy from it. Panic took hold of her, welling again inside as she held her breath, unaware of the silent appeal in her eyes as she clung to Chris's gaze.

When he spoke his voice was like ice. 'If this is Denton again are you going to speak to him?'

'Chris—'

'Right! Then if you're not, I will! After all, I'll need to know what he intends to do with Tregarn if he comes back on the scene.' Chris turned abruptly and was through the door and picking up the phone before Hannah had time to stop him. With her heart in her mouth she listened as his voice cracked down the phone. 'Yes, who is this?'

Relief flooded over her as she heard his, *'Oh, it's you, Steve,'* his tone quieter as he recognized the caller as someone other than Paul Denton.

Hannah sank back on to the sofa. She could still hear Chris's muted tones coming from the hall, just loud enough for her to hear. He was making some kind of arrangement for the twenty-fifth.

Then the talk veered to something else,

126

something she could barely comprehend and, suddenly, her heart froze as his words began to sink in.

'No, Steve, like I said, I won't be coming by myself. What? Certainly I'm hoping my wife will be with me . . .'

She heard his wry laugh at some comment from the man called Steve, then he went on, *'Yes, that's true enough.'* Another short silence, then, *'What? Of course I still feel the same way about her. I know it's been a long time but I'll sort it out, don't you worry.'*

The conversation changed course. Now they were talking about horses but Hannah couldn't move. She sat quite still, numbed by Chris's words. She heard the click as he put the phone down and her glazed eyes looked up as he came back into the room.

'Now, to get back to what we were saying— you were just about to explain.'

Hannah opened her mouth to speak but no words came. A knock on the door distracted them both and Megan's head bobbed round.

'Yes, Megan, what is it?' Chris sounded impatient.

'Excuse me, Chris, but Mickey's told me to tell you the colt's arrived and you're wanted at the stables right away.'

'Right, tell him I'm on my way.' He turned back to Hannah as she sat very still. 'We'll talk about this tonight. I want to know exactly what's going on.' He moved to the door, turning back as he reached it. 'I'd like to meet this Denton fellow—he must be quite a man.'

Hannah looked back numbly then he was gone. She remained where she was for a long time, not moving, and her brain hardly comprehending what she'd overheard.

My wife will be with me!

What a fool she'd been. What an idiot to even think for one moment that he loved her! He had never loved her! She should have known better! Hannah buried her head in her hands, too hurt and too shocked even to cry.

At last she stirred. She couldn't stand it any longer! Even a worm will turn when it was pushed too far. Her limit had been reached. She was tired of it all and, getting up slowly, she stood quietly for a moment deciding what to do. A little while later she went out into the hall, her eyes running along the row of telephone directories until she found the one she wanted.

Hannah dialled the nearest car rental company, speaking briefly to the clipped, professional voice at the other end, and the Fiat was delivered in less than an hour.

Upstairs, in her room, she flung her few possessions into the suitcases then, unlocking the Fiat, she threw them into the boot.

'Where are you going?'

Hannah looked towards the voice. Megan was standing in the doorway.

'I'm going home, Megan. Back where I

belong.'

Without another glance, Hannah drove away, her blue eyes glittering with tears. She gritted her teeth as she reached the main road and manoeuvred the car into the flow of traffic, wincing inwardly as she remembered how close she'd been to telling Chris of her love. Why, he would have laughed in her face! He was going back to Joyce! He had always loved Joyce!

The summer was dying now, and the leaves were beginning to fall to earth like tiny birds, helpless in the wind. Since she'd been a little girl—whenever trouble threatened—she had scurried back to Tregarn, steeping herself in its tranquillity and letting it wrap around her like a comfortable old cloak. Always, the sight of Tregarn's familiar, honey-stone walls brought back a deep-rooted sense of safety; an anchorage filled with well-remembered memories of people, scents, places and laughter; memories of times when people loved her.

Now everything had changed! The phone call from Chris's friend Steve had seen to that! She had to clear up this mess with Paul and— by going back to him—she would guarantee Chris Talbot's safety. She would owe him nothing!

CHAPTER TEN

Tregarn was deserted, there wasn't a soul about and Hannah parked the Fiat directly in front of the house, switching off the engine, winding down the window and leaning back in the seat. She breathed in the air and listened to the sound of the birds in the trees around her.

Her eyes focused on her old home. It seemed almost a stranger to her now; no longer an integral part of her life. It had always been at its glorious best in the autumn and, outwardly, apart from the annexe and the new glass extensions that made up the souvenir, craft and garden shops, it hadn't changed that much. It sat silently proud amidst its wide canopy of trees and, climbing out of the car, Hannah walked slowly up the newly surfaced steps, running a nervous hand along its honey-stoned balustrade.

Well, she'd kept her promise—Tregarn would survive. Yet, standing there, Hannah suddenly felt an overwhelming tide of desolation flow over her, remembering with a sudden nostalgic longing, the happier times when she had been small, and she had believed the world to be her oyster.

Tregarn seemed to have drawn away from her. As if it was trying to tell her something—

that it didn't need her any more. That the time had come for them both to move on and, in the spring, when the house opened its doors to a new beginning, it wanted no part of the past, and Hannah must look elsewhere for her happiness.

Her slender fingers shook a little as she unlocked the door and flipped the catch so that it wouldn't lock again, leaving easy access for Paul, and saying a little prayer to herself that he wouldn't leave it too long before he came.

She moved warily along the corridor. The smell of fresh paint was everywhere, bringing on a nauseous feeling in her stomach and she was glad of the breeze that came through an open window high in a recess.

It was all very quiet. Hannah reached her father's old study and, as she opened the door, the sunlight dazzled her eyes, sending things she knew almost as well as her own face, into deep, dark shadows.

The oak floors had been left bare, polished to a warm, glowing lustre and Hannah found it hard to picture the study as it had once been, slightly shabby and always with that familiar musty odour. Now, the trendy new furniture jumped sharply into her focus.

She walked over to the desk, running her fingers along its restored surface, and her heart gave a lurch as her thoughts flooded back to Chris. She remembered that first rainy

131

night when she discussed the twenty-four acres of land; the night when he'd made it impossible for her to love any other man—or belong to anyone but him.

With an impatient toss of her dark head she tried again to thrust him out of her mind. He was out of her life now, and nothing would ever bring him back. And, besides, it was pointless wishing for the moon when it was out of her reach.

She had other things to do. She must concentrate on the future—*her* future—and leave Christian Langley Talbot to rebuild his life with the woman he had chosen—his wife!

It was over. He didn't belong to her! And, looking back, she realized sadly that he never really had.

Methodically, she looked around, forcing her attention on her surroundings. The next few hours would be crucial and she had to prepare herself. She had to be ready to meet Paul.

She sat herself down at her father's desk and waited. This afternoon, Paul had said. Well, it was almost evening already. While she waited she prayed fervently that she wasn't pushing her luck. Oddly, she wasn't afraid for herself. She had been through so much at Paul's hands, one way or another, that she simply wasn't afraid of him any more. But she was terribly afraid for Chris. She knew the venom of Paul's jealousy and, even though

132

Chris Talbot was no longer a part of her life, she couldn't allow Paul to harm him.

The minutes passed, they became an hour—then two. She hoped again she was doing the right thing. Perhaps she should have telephoned the police. But what could she have told them? That she was going home? That there was a madman making threats because he wanted her back?

The sky began to take on the first signs of evening. Cold feelings were washing across her thoughts and, just as Hannah was thinking that perhaps Paul had changed his mind after all, her heart almost stopped as the door slowly opened and he walked in.

'Hello, Paul.'

He looked a little thinner than the last time she'd seen him, and his hair seemed darker. But the eyes looked just the same. Too cold, too intense.

He didn't answer for a long time then he said 'Hannah' in a curious voice; so quiet that she almost couldn't hear him. He looked around the study, his eyes flickering to the window and then back to the door. He stepped back, turning the key, then turned back to Hannah, saying in that same curious tone, 'You look well—lovely as always.'

Hannah nodded gravely. 'Thank you, Paul. Hasn't the summer been hot?' What a remarkably silly thing to say. Deep inside herself she recognized the first awful signs of

133

hysteria and fought to check them as Paul continued to stare at her in that strange feverish manner.

'Why did you move in with Chris Talbot?'

The sudden lash of fury in his voice made Hannah jump and, as her glance darted to his face, the look in his pale eyes sent her heart thumping against her ribs. His expression was hideous. His mouth had twisted in the way she remembered and she felt sick to her stomach.

She swallowed, managing to say with creditable calm, 'He offered to put me up until Tregarn was finished.'

'Stop lying to me! You're living with him, aren't you?'

Cold panic was spreading over her now and she swallowed again, trying desperately not to show Paul any of her fears. 'Not in the way you think, Paul. And it was over between us anyway.'

He shook his head slowly, his eyes narrowing to slits. 'You are the one who says that—I don't!'

Hannah recognized the signs. He was building himself up into a fury—a rage that would not be controlled until he released it on her in all its violence. 'We both agreed, don't you remember?' she reminded him softly, trying to diffuse his temper. 'It was the best thing for you when you fell in love with your present girl—it was what you seemed to want.' She broke off, terrified now as he leapt from his chair, knocking it over with his movement.

His hand moved swiftly to his inside pocket and he brought out a gun. 'She was nothing! And don't patronize me!'

Utter calmness was Hannah's only weapon. It was a pitiful defence but it was all she had. 'Paul . . . please . . . don't be silly. Put that gun away.'

A cold smile touched his mouth. Paul was ill—truly ill. 'No one else will have my wife.'

'Paul.' Hannah couldn't move. Her eyes were glued to the barrel of his gun as he levelled it towards her, 'Paul . . . it's not doing any good trying to scare me like this. We can work something out . . . I . . .'

'It's too late! And if I can't have you, nobody will!' Slowly he brought the gun level with her forehead. 'I've worked it all out for myself—no one's going to stop me.' He sneered, a malicious sneer that curled his mouth. The old, bitter look was on his face and he seemed to withdraw into himself as he spoke again, his tone curiously flat. 'First you . . . then Talbot. He should have got my message by now.'

'*Message?*'

He laughed. 'Yes. I've sent him a note as though it's from you.' He laughed again, an ugly sound. 'But by the time he gets here, he will be too late.' The harsh laughter died and his face hardened into a cruel mask. 'And, my inconstant Hannah, that will be the end of

135

both of you—I'll be waiting for him.'

At once Hannah knew what he planned to do. Somehow, she had to prevent this terrible thing and she raised a trembling placating hand. 'Why, Paul?' she whispered. 'Why must you hurt either of us? Chris hasn't done anything. He was only helping me out. He hasn't tried to take me away from you if that's what you think.' She was desperate now. 'No one could do that.' Somehow, she had to win Paul over, at least long enough to put the gun out of harm's way. She felt she was groping through a spider's web, seeing only darkness. In a shaky voice she went on, 'I'll—I'll come back to you, Paul.'

A brief look of triumph flashed into his eyes and, seeing it, Hannah gathered her strength, her words rushing out now like a torrent. 'I'll even get married to you again if that's what you want, but . . . please don't hurt me or Chris.'

Paul's face had turned deathly white now and there was no doubt about his reaction to her offer. It was only momentary triumph, it was also stupefaction! He glared at her across the desk, the gun still levelled perilously at her head. 'Are you crazy? Do you think I could touch you now after he's had his hands on you? Never! Never! It's time—'

Suddenly, everything went crazy! All hell seemed to break loose as the door crashed open, propelled by something that took it clear off its hinges. Paul twisted furiously towards the sound and, seizing her chance, Hannah grabbed her father's glass ash-tray from the desk and hurled it towards him. It hit its mark, thudding against his arm and sending the revolver clattering to the ground. The crack of it deafened her as he'd tried to fire it towards the door.

Hannah screamed as two burly figures leapt from the blackness of the doorway, the heavier one taking Paul with a tackle that sent him crashing to the ground. Shouts and curses were everywhere, then came the sound of wood splintering as another shot thudded into it.

Instinctively, Hannah ducked, crouching low behind the desk, her hands against her ears and screaming Chris's name over and over again. She had recognized his great strength as he'd sent Paul spinning to the floor. Now, close by her, came the sickening sounds of men fighting and, scrambling to her feet, she made blindly for the door. Someone grabbed her, making soothing sounds and, as she looked back into the chaos of the room, she found she was sobbing into the arms of a policeman. She lifted up her head again, looking across the room to see that Chris was straddled over Paul, his face a mask of white fury at the man who'd tried to harm her.

'Please!' Hannah freed herself from the policeman's restraint and rushed forward to throw herself against Chris. Tears streamed

137

down her face and she threw her arms around his neck, holding him back. 'He's ill, Chris . . . he's ill . . .'

Chris froze, her words reaching him and, after a few frozen seconds, his hands fell to his side. He got to his feet, hauling her up and holding her until she felt she could hardly breathe. Then she wept uncontrollably as she felt his arms close even tighter around her, his whispered words a choked mixture of half comfort and half curses.

Soon the room seemed to fill with policemen. Two of them led Paul out, and he passed her with a strange unrecognizing look in his eyes—as if he didn't know who she was any more. Hannah wept again—perhaps he didn't.

'Are you OK?'

Hannah lifted her face to Chris. He looked like a man who'd been to hell and back, his dark eyes preoccupied and serious. When she nodded he looked at her for a few moments longer then he glanced away.

She looked at him, her face pale and strained. 'How did you know Paul would be here?'

'He sent me a note—I knew it wasn't from you. I rang the police. They knew who he was—they were looking for him, too, about your car. And they were looking for a stolen gun—thought he might have been a terrorist.' Hannah saw a muscle twitching in his throat as

138

he went on, 'Never dreamed he was a jealous husband out to hurt his ex-wife.'

'He's ill.' Hannah's legs seemed to have lost all their strength and she leaned against Chris for support. Her head was swimming and black mists were swirling around her brain.

'Here, drink this.' Chris's voice came from far away as Hannah gulped something down. It was a spirit of some kind and, as it burned inside her, she let the relaxing warmth of the drink flow through her bones. She could still hear Chris talking to her from that same, far-away place. 'You could have been killed. Didn't you know it was the same man who tried to run you off the road?'

'I know, you came just in time,' she answered softly, barely breathing. 'But how did you know about the accident?'

'The police told me. And I thought something queer was going on when the garage started to ask questions about the state of your car. Why didn't you tell me about it?'

Hannah shivered, but she wasn't cold. 'I thought I could handle it. I didn't want you to be involved in more of my problems.' She looked up at him. He looked as if he hadn't slept in a week, or shaved or combed his hair. Half the buttons of his blue shirt were undone and his jeans were badly creased, as though he hadn't taken them off for years. 'You look awful.'

His lips twisted into a wry smile. 'Thanks for

the vote of confidence.' He looked at her for a moment longer, then said quietly, 'I've lost twenty years of my life today. When Megan told me that you'd come back here—I thought I would go crazy and I wasn't sure you were worth it.' Hannah didn't reply as his eyes swept over her. 'I've already met Paul Denton. Now, where can I find boy-friend number two—Mr Wonderful?'

'What are you saying, Chris?' she asked quietly.

'Oh, for goodness sake!' he exclaimed with savage impatience. 'I'm saying that I've almost had World War Three with Paul and yet there's still the other man you say you're in love with.' He stared at her balefully, his eyes locked into hers and his face taut with anger. With deliberate coldness he added bitterly, 'It's Mr Wonderful that I'm concerned about now.'

Hannah tried to wrest back her emotions. She stood watching him, her eyes huge and the fingertips of her left hand pressed up against her lips, as if to stem the tide of words that threatened to rush out. She turned away, her eyes sweeping over the wrecked study. 'You're always too concerned about me, Chris. Right from the start you've helped me.' She smiled ruefully before she continued, 'That's been the trouble. You've helped me with Tregarn—I couldn't have done it on my own, I know that now. You gave me your home, comfort, care

140

and concern, and I've put you under considerable strain today with Paul. I'm sorry, Chris, for everything.'

His eyes as he looked at her were bloodshot and swollen. Inside, she raged that Paul could cause such havoc as this and she gritted her teeth against the wave of anger that swept over her as she looked at his battered face. A feeling of anger primitive and protective, flooded through her as she looked up at the legacy of Paul's deranged attack.

'I don't want to talk about "Mr Wonderful", Chris,' she murmured quietly, a lump forming in her throat. 'He has no part in my life.'

For a few seconds he stared at her, his expression blank, then, his voicc deadly quiet, he demanded, 'Tell me about him!'

In the lengthening silence she felt his determination to know all the answers. Half-formed thoughts whirled around in her brain, then settled into a meaningless disorder of which she could make no sense. She whispered finally, 'Why should you be interested? What diff—'

His voice seared as he broke in, 'Because I *am* interested! Now tell me!'

Her eyes flew to his face. Chilled by the remorseless set of his features, she whispered, 'But why? What good would it do now?'

He lunged forward and grabbed her arms, his face tight with rage. 'Tell me!'

Suddenly Hannah wanted to laugh—really

laugh—at the irony of it all. Chris Talbot was her heart and soul, more important to her than life itself. She loved him! But how could she tell him that he was the root cause of all the unhappiness in her life? 'You are the last person I could tell,' she choked, the blood drained from her cheeks. 'I'm sorry, Chris.'

He sighed tiredly. 'Don't be sorry, put it down to experience. I could do with a drink.'

Hannah permitted herself a small smile. 'Sorry, all out I'm afraid.'

'I can wait until we're back home.'

Hannah looked at him with a clear steadying gaze, taking a quick fortifying breath. 'Home? We?'

'It's been a long day,' he answered calmly.

'I'm home already, remember? This is my home.'

He stared into her eyes for a long time before asking incredulously, 'You're surely not planning on staying here, are you?'

Hannah felt the walls closing in on her again, stifling her. She stood bolt upright, her eyes riveted on his face. 'Of course I am. I—I'll never come back to Twr Gwyn.'

Chris looked at her dumbstruck, his eyes puzzled and more than a little impatient. 'What do you mean?' he asked in a deadly quiet voice.

'I can never go back there, not now.'

'Well, you can't stay here.'

'Yes, I can.'

'And where will you sleep? There isn't a room fitted out with beds yet. What do you plan to do—kip down in here?' He circled his arm, indicating the stark furniture and the uncarpeted floor. 'And apart from that, what will you do for food?'

'I'll find something.'

'Oh, I see.' His tone was scathing now. 'You're planning on becoming a new tourist attraction, are you? The Wild Woman of Tregarn!' His dark eyes glared, hard and brilliant, as he stared down at her. 'You're coming back to Twr Gwyn with me!'

Hot colour burned her cheeks. 'You can't *force* me to leave here.'

'You'll do exactly as I tell you.'

He moved forward swiftly, and when his arms came around her it was too much to bear. She wanted to forget everything; Joyce, Paul, Tregarn. She wanted to shut the world out and just let him support her forever with his hard strength.

'Come on, stop being stubborn. You're coming with me whether you like it or not.'

His voice was full of confidence now and, keeping a firm hold, he marched her outside to the Shogun, pushing her in and driving like a demon back to Twr Gwyn without another word.

CHAPTER ELEVEN

Chris still gripped his hand tightly around her arm as they went into the house. Without a word to anyone, including Megan who stood in the hallway watching them with lifted brows, he led her straight through to the sitting-room, opening the door, pushing her gently but firmly through and kicking it shut behind him.

'Now, tell me why you've so suddenly decided to go back to Tregarn?' he demanded in a voice that told her it would take no more nonsense.

Hannah raised her blue eyes to meet the cold dark eyes of the man she loved. 'Because,' she acknowledged calmly, 'I can't stay here when you bring Joyce back.'

Chris studied her through narrowed eyes. 'Have you lost your marbles?'

She lowered her head, unwilling to meet his astonished scrutiny unless he read too much in her own. 'I can't stay here,' she began tremulously. 'Not any more—not without—'

He moved away from her. 'Without . . . what?' he broke in raggedly. 'Without *love*. Is that what you're finding so hard to say?'

'How can I stay here now? How can I make Twr Gwyn my home without—' She made an attempt at a wan smile. 'Yes, I'll admit it . . . love?'

His face was cold and withdrawn as he jerked his head to look at her. 'I've been asking myself that same question for weeks.'

Hannah moistened her lips, her heart pounding against her ribs. 'It's bad enough being here when I know everybody believes that I share your bed. But to stay here now . . . now that Joyce—'

She broke off, words failing her. She wanted to go out of this affair with as much dignity as she could but even now, standing with only the few feet separating them, he was already tearing away at her insides.

He moved towards her, cupping her face in his hands and forcing her pain-filled eyes to meet his. He spoke softly, barely audible, bringing his lips to her forehead and kissing her slowly. His touch drew a response from her that shocked and frightened her. How on earth was she going to live her life without this man?

'Hannah,' he whispered. 'Hannah, when are you going to stop tearing the guts out of me?'

'No, no, Chris, don't,' she cried, struggling for sanity. 'I've got to go, can't you understand? I've told you, I can't stay here when you bring Joyce back! I can't even stay at Tregarn! I'm selling it! I'm going away!'

'Going away? What are you talking about? And what's Joyce got to do with any of this?'

'I heard you . . . on the phone.' She pushed herself away, facing up to him, 'I heard you telling your friend Steve that you were hoping to be back with your wife on the—the twenty-fifth.'

He snatched her up against him again. 'I could kill you for scaring me like that,' he muttered. 'We're getting married right away, before your imagination sends the pair of us crazy—and before your invisible Mr Wonderful comes back to throw in his two pennyworth.'

Abruptly, she lifted her head and gave him an unbelieving stare. She felt as if she could no longer breathe. Married? How could she possibly marry him? Unless . . . Her heart pounded again, hopeful, incredulous. She was bewildered, confused. 'But—'

'Don't you like the idea? Heaven knows, I do.'

'How can I?' Her face was white now in its mask of surprise. 'Joyce—'

He reached out for her again, pulling her close. 'You've got it all wrong. All I've ever wanted is to love you and for you to love me. When you heard me on the phone talking about my wife, I meant you, Hannah. I was counting on it. Steve knows how long I've waited for you—he even put a bet on it—he didn't think I had a chance. I vowed that I would ask you to be my wife and take you to his place for dinner—and I still hope to. It was you I was talking about. I'd hoped by then that I'd have persuaded you to like me enough to marry me.' He looked down at her with hungry fire in his dark eyes. 'Do you like me enough to marry me?'

Hannah felt her muscles contract as Chris bent his head to kiss her. 'But I thought . . .'

'I know now what you thought, and you're wrong—dead wrong.'

Her breath made a sighing sound through her teeth as her eyes searched his for a sign of insincerity. There was none. 'So I misunderstood? I thought you were talking about Joyce, that you were hoping for a reconciliation.'

His face was grim. 'It was over between us a long time ago. It was the biggest mistake of my life—and hers too, as it turned out. She told me she was pregnant, and I, like a fool, believed her. I did the honourable thing and married her.' His mouth hardened into a bitter line. 'She wasn't pregnant after all, and after less than a year of the country life, she found it wasn't her style. She left me for some chap she met on one of her frequent trips back to Ireland.'

'I'm so sorry, Chris.'

Chris spoke without emphasis but his voice had the flatness of a hammer on steel. 'Don't be. I was relieved when it happened. We got a divorce quickly and that was the end of that.'

'But I thought . . .' Hannah put out her hand in a little futile gesture. 'When you went to Ireland, I thought you'd gone to see her.'

Chris laughed, the sound seductive. 'So

147

that's what it was. I wondered what the inquisition was about when I got back.' His eyes rested on her tenderly. 'You little goose, I went to Ireland to buy a colt . . .' His mouth curved teasingly. 'And, I'll admit, to stay with a woman.'

Hannah jerked her head, her eyes widening and her heart thumping painfully. 'A woman?'

'Yes . . . my mother.'

She gasped. 'Your mother? But—but, I always thought your mother had died when we were children.'

'No, mum's alive and well, and running a stable in Killarney. I bought the new colt from her. A couple of years after my dad died she found some good-looking Irishman and scooted off to marry him.'

Hannah felt a great surge of love rise in her heart. 'It must—it must have been an awful time for you when Joyce left you,' she said quietly.

'It was, but not in the way you're thinking. The only awful part when it happened to me was, I loved someone else—always had. And I didn't know how I was ever going to be able to show my love.' He reached out his hand and stroked her hair, and when Hannah opened her mouth to speak he made a silencing gesture. 'Let me get this out of my system. You may not believe this,' he went on quietly, looking at her with such tenderness that it almost made her cry. 'And I wouldn't blame

148

you if you didn't. But all those years when we've been apart, every time I got close to another woman, I saw your face. I wanted my marriage to work because I felt so guilty about it. I wanted to feel for her what I'd always felt for you, but I never could. Perhaps that's why she looked for someone else.' He cleared his throat then went on in an unsteady voice. 'And just before you came back—before your father died—I promised him . . .'

'My father?'

'Ssh.'

Hannah kept silent, her breathing becoming an effort. She'd waited such a long time to hear things and now that she was, it all seemed so unreal, a dream. 'I promised him that I would take care of you. Your dad was an astute old man, he always believed we would be together some day. But when you started going out with Paul Denton and seemed so settled, he thought it was what you wanted.' Chris chuckled softly. 'He didn't give up though. He made me promise that if I ever got the opportunity to take you away from him, I would. I gave that promise gladly.'

'You and Dad conspired against Paul and I?'

'Hannah, let me finish, there's still more. I never owned those twenty-four acres you know.'

'*What* did you say?'

'I'd only leased them from your father and

149

when I knew you wanted them for your bungalows, well, it was the answer to my prayers. I had to find a way of making you stay so that I could get to know you a little better. I had to know if my instincts had been right all along, and that there really was a warm woman beneath that snooty surface.' He gave a small, lop-sided grin. 'This is tough,' he said. 'Telling you these things is one of the toughest things I've ever had to do . . . you've always acted like you hated me, as if there was a smell about me.'

Hannah's blue eyes regarded him with a hint of bitterness. 'That was my protection against you,' she said huskily. 'You scared me to death. I knew I'd be lost with a man like you. I was glad in a way that you never looked at me twice.'

'Never looked?' Chris laughed harshly. 'I looked more than twice, believe me. And every time I did, you tied my gut in a knot.'

Her lips trembled. 'And I thought you didn't like me.'

He bent forward, kissing her lightly on the tip of her nose. 'That must be the most misleading thought of all time.' His face became more sombre as he went on, 'What I'm trying to say, and not very well, is to tell you how I feel.'

Instinctively, she raised her face to meet his mouth. She loved him so much and now she didn't care what he said or did anymore.

Remembering that, she whispered against his cheek, 'You always were a tricky devil, Talbot.'

He smiled a little sheepishly and pressed his lips against her forehead, 'Yes, I was, wasn't I? But I've still not finished. There's something else I have to get off my chest . . .'

'Still more?'

'Your dad insisted I use those twenty-four acres—he had no use for them when he sold his cattle.' He smiled again faintly, watching the dawning horror in her expression with amusement. 'Now don't get mad. When I refused to *sell* them back to you, it was because it was the only excuse I could think of to keep you here.'

He moved to take her in his arms. 'Of all the low down, dirty tricks.'

He smiled, his voice husky and his lips against her cheek. 'Working on the annexe, getting you to stay at Twr Gwyn, was the only way I knew to give me time to get you to love me.'

'I've always loved you, Chris,' she whispered, her lips brushing his.

She felt him stiffen. For a few seconds, realization held him still. Then, as his eyes probed her face and his arms gripped her tightly. 'Say that again.'

Hannah held his gaze, her eyes bright now. 'I've always loved you.'

'But you said you'd always loved this other—this mystery man.'

151

'You fool, Chris. You are the invisible Mr Wonderful. It was you I meant. You were always the only man in my life, even Paul knew that. That's why it all went so wrong with him. But I thought you despised me as a person— that you were only interested in my body. And you can't blame me for that, can you, knowing your reputation? And, even over these last weeks when we've been together so much, you've never once given the slightest hint that you cared for me.'

'Good Lord, surely you could see that every time I looked at you? Everyone else could see it! I'm sick of the cracks I've had to take about when I would win you over—from Megan, the chaps, yes, and even old Galbraith.'

'I hoped—sometimes, I thought perhaps— but I was never sure.'

Chris pulled her effortlessly against him. 'Are you sure now?'

'Yes, oh yes,' she whispered.

She was safe in his arms now, the most precious part of his world. She had been wrong about him, just as she had been wrong about so many things. Things like her feelings for Paul; the lies she'd believed about Chris; so many, many things.

His arms tightened around her, seeing the shadows that had crept into her eyes. He tilted her head again, kissing her gently. 'I love you, Hannah Jones.'

The clouds faded. 'And I love you, too.'

How wonderful it was to say those words! And as if that wasn't enough happiness for her to bear, Tregarn was safe as well. Tregarn and Twr Gwyn!

'But Chris, what about Tregarn?'

Half serious, half amused, he returned, 'Tregarn? What about it?'

Almost afraid to ask, she said, 'Do you think it will be a success?'

He grinned. 'How can it fail? Which reminds me, I have another small confession to make.'

'Not another?'

'I'm afraid so. I never signed my half of the contract—never intended to. It's still yours, every inch of it. The money I put in as an investment was only what I'd owed your dad all these years for the use of his land.'

She glanced at him quickly, a slow smile forming her mouth. 'You really take the biscuit in the dirty tricks department. But—' she paused a moment to swallow the constriction in her throat, '—Tregarn isn't entirely mine any more, it's *ours* Chris—it belongs to both of us.'

Chris grinned. 'And who's going to run it? Would you like the job—at least, until the children come along? You could always dust the roses. And if you play your cards right, I may even let you handle the riding-school side of it—you haven't done a bad job on my horses.'

She slapped him playfully. 'No thanks, you're too bossy, we'll run it together.'

'We'll re-name it—Twr Tregarn—how about that?'

'Tregarn Twr sounds better.'

He laughed, pulling her into the crook of his shoulder. 'We'll get married by special licence tomorrow. After all, it's barely three days to the twenty-fifth and I wouldn't let Steve down for a gold clock.'

'How much was the bet by the way?'

'Fifty pence. Now tell me again that you love me.'

The sun came into her eyes as Hannah kissed him, whispering, 'I love you . . .'